Mariposa

Treacherous

Butterfly

Carmella Savona

Mariposa Treacherous Butterfly

Copyright © 2024 Carmella Savona

All Rights Reserved

Dedication

To my little Brother Nick, I am so proud of the man you have become. The courage it has taken for you to overcome your demons and be steadfast in your sobriety is inspiring. I have admired your ability to never compromise who you are or what you want in terms of love; you are always looking for ways to improve yourself so you can be the best version for someone else. I love you!

Acknowledgment

First and foremost, thank you to my readers, those who have supported me and anxiously await the conclusion of this trilogy. I am excited to deliver Mariposa, book two, and happy to say that book three, Free to Fly, will be the hot and spicy conclusion to Treacherous Butterfly.

A special thanks to those who have inspired me. To The Stixxx, Joe and Syni, together you two have created music that reflects a journey of struggle, triumph, and truth. I was fortunate enough to meet both of you and experience a very small portion of your synergy in a short amount of time, but I have always followed your progress. The both of you are the embodiment of resilience and staying true to yourselves, which has inspired me to create some of the characters in this book. But most of all, watching you has taught me to hustle harder and follow my dreams.

I wish you both nothing but the best and success. If only I had a dragon to fly us all to the top.

Thank you to my uncle, Shane, for always wanting the best for me, although I do not believe that the best will ever exist when it comes to the women you love. You are the husband that women dream of: handsome, present, successful, and loyal. It's a hard combination to find.

Your marriage to Aunt Tish is an inspiration and a testament to the power of partnership.

And a special thanks to Aunt Tish: food is our love language, and you have kept Grandma's spirit alive with your amazing meals, simple or feast; they reflect your love and dedication to this family.

Contents

Dedication 3

Acknowledgment 4

About the Author 7

Chapter 1 8

Chapter 2 18

Chapter 3 26

Chapter 4 35

Chapter 5 43

Chapter 6 50

Chapter 7 57

Chapter 8 68

Chapter 9 76

Chapter 10 83

Chapter 11 90

Chapter 12 96

Chapter 13 105

Chapter 14 113

Chapter 15 122

Chapter 16 131

Chapter 17 142

Chapter 18 153

Chapter 19 167

Chapter 20 185

About the Author

Carmella Savona grew up in Macon, GA, 80 miles south of Atlanta, GA. She works with individuals with an array of disabilities and mental health disorders but has always had a passion for writing. This will be her second book, a three-part series of a suspenseful romance and the path to true love. Please visit her website: http://Carmellasavona.com

Chapter 1

Seven Years Earlier

Wednesday

Mateo sat at his computer, deeply focused on researching a variety of cleaning supplies. He was looking at different resources to find the top-rated products and scents that would transform any home into a pristine sanctuary, mirroring the impeccable cleanliness and inviting fragrance of his own living space.

As he scrolled through countless reviews, he thought about how happy he was. MC Cleaning Services was doing pretty well, thanks to his combined efforts, Camille's, and a team of reliable employees. Their hard work paved the way for Mateo's success, and he could finally glimpse the realization of his dreams for a legitimate life in the States.

"Hey, Cami, come over here. I want to show you something," Mateo called out to Camille from the other room.

Cami poked her head around the corner, her black hair adorned with smudges of dye around the edges of her forehead. "What is it, sweetheart? I've got dye on my roots and really need to wash it out," she replied with a hint of urgency in her voice.

Mateo chuckled. "Why don't you go to the salon and take care of that?"

"You know I don't like spending money like that," Cami retorted, pursing her lips. "It's just a few gray hairs that need touching up." She added, pointing to her head.

Mateo reclined in his chair, a playful smirk dancing across his lips. "I appreciate your frugality, but our business is thriving. I was just looking at the numbers, and we're making a sizable profit. Besides, I have more than enough for you to enjoy a day at the salon. Cami, mi amor, you don't have to worry about money anymore."

Cami gazed at Mateo with adoration in her eyes. "This business can't be making that much money this early on. I just want to save where we can. We have two apartments, overhead for the business, cars, equipment... If I can handle it myself, then so be it. But right now, I really need to wash this out, or I won't have any hair left," she reasoned urgently.

Mateo chuckled at the image of Cami with a bald head. "Please, Amor, go wash your hair and come back in here. I have an idea."

Cami hurried to the bathroom, washing her long, silky black hair. After shuffling it with a towel, she made her way back to the makeshift office in Mateo's bedroom. She lightly settled onto his lap, her soft skin irresistible to him. Mateo's hands moved slowly down her legs, nestling his face in her neck. Cami giggled at his lack of control when he touched her. "Tell me what your idea is. We can play later," she teased.

Mateo's hands retreated, and he focused on his idea. "Well, since our employees have done so well, we should show them how much we appreciate them. I thought about calling that nice new bar downtown and renting out the VIP section."

Cami furrowed her brow in wonder. "Where are you getting all this money? We've invested so much in this business, not to mention our personal bills. Why not just a nice dinner or a bonus for the employees?"

Mateo swiveled his office chair, deliberately avoiding her question, which forced Cami to stand up. He fixed his gaze on the computer screen, pretending to be searching for VIP packages at the swankiest places in town. Cami's frustration grew. "Why do you always dodge my questions about money? It drives me crazy. Did you win the lottery and forget to tell me? Inherit a fortune? Rob a bank? I mean, seriously, Mateo, I know you think I'm cheap, but I just can't justify blowing that kind of cash."

Mateo remained unresponsive, his attention fixed on the screen, causing Cami to stomp her feet in anger and storm out of the room. As she left, Mateo softly uttered, "Some things are better left unanswered."

Friday

Cami entered the room, her leopard skin dress and black stiletto heels captivating Mateo. "You are stunning, Amor," he murmured as Cami wrapped her arms around him. Yet, disappointment was etched on her face. "Are you sure you don't want to go? You're leaving me to entertain our staff, and you won't even be there. This was your bright idea, by the way."

Mateo responded with a light kiss. "I have work to do. I don't drink, and the thought of loud music and a bunch of drunks does not excite me. Besides, I've put Felix in charge tonight. He'll be looking out for you. I gave him one of my phones to take with him so he can reach me in case of an emergency."

Cami laughed, puzzled. "I don't understand you and all these cell phones. Just call him on his phone. I'm sure he wants to have fun and not have to keep up with that phone all night."

Mateo dismissed her concern. "Felix is fine with it. You let me worry about that. You'll have the VIP section at Titans nightclub, a driver set up, food, champagne—the whole ten yards," he said, unaware of his mistake.

"You mean the whole nine yards," Cami corrected, chuckling. Mateo tilted his head, not fully grasping the expression but noting the correction nonetheless.

"I still don't understand where all this money comes from, but I'm going to quit asking and enjoy myself. I'm tired of trying to figure it out," Cami declared, recalling her friend Julia's suspicions.

Mateo handed her an envelope of cash. "Don't spend it all in one place," he joked, watching Cami roll her eyes as she muttered, "This is exactly the kind of thing I'm talking about," before leaving Mateo behind.

7:00 PM

Mateo dialed his trusted employee and friend, Felix. "Hola, ¿Qué pasa, güey? (Hello, what's up, buddy?)" Felix responded in a hurried tone, "Waiting for Cami. Is everything okay?"

"Yeah, everything's okay. I wanted to make sure you have the phone on. I'm meeting someone later; I'm unsure about this guy. He's coming in from Florida. We have to make an exchange, but I don't have a good feeling," Mateo stated, his words evident with concern.

"Do you want me to stay back and assist with the exchange? I can have Leo watch over Cami. There will be 6 others with her; she'll be okay with them, I'm sure of it," Felix stated.

Mateo hesitated, pondering the thought. "No, it will be fine. I trust you, and besides, you have helped us so much with the business. Go have some fun. Just keep the phone on," Mateo stated hesitantly, defying his better judgment for assistance.

11:30 PM

Gabriella and Rowen were enjoying the peace of the apartment with her little brothers. Her mother was off, entertaining the staff of MC cleaning services. Sneaking a bottle of wine from her mother's treasured cheap wine collection, the two sat on the balcony, sipping away like southern aristocrats in a grand mansion.

"Are you gay, Rowen?" Gabriella bluntly questioned.

Rowen took a swig of his wine while his pinkie finger drifted away from the glass. "I don't know, Gabs, maybe. Like, I do find men attractive. Does that make me gay?" Rowen said, questioning his own sexuality.

"Rowen, you have fully bathed me after a night of puking, butt ass naked, like you were one of my girlfriends and never seemed a bit impressed by my naked body. Honestly, I feel like you are a girl."

The two teenagers laughed, but it was cut short by loud banging on the door and a light muffle.

"Do you hear that?" Rowen asked, "Sounds like someone groaning or something. Oh God, Gabby, I'm scared. Should we call the police?"

Gabriella's forever brave spirit makes her way to the door, looking out the peephole to see nothing.

Gabriella jumped back as knocking sounded at the bottom of the door. "Oh my God, Rowen, who could it be? They're knocking on the bottom of the door. That's not normal, is it?" she exclaimed.

Rowen joined her on the floor, listening to the moans and muffled voices of someone from the other side of the door. It sounded like the person, whoever it was, was in pain and could barely speak. Gabriella whispered to Rowen, "Is that Mateo?" At that moment, a weary voice called out Gabriella's name, pleading, "Por favor, puerta."

Gabriella leaped to her feet and opened the door, followed by a scream. There on the concrete lay Mateo, covered in blood and barely breathing.

"Rowen, call the police, hurry! I am going to call my mother," Gabriella urged as she attempted to drag Mateo into the apartment. Rowen quickly dialed 911 as Gabriella struggled to help Mateo inside. Mateo slowly pulled a phone from his pocket, blood covering the broken screen. He pointed to a contact: Felix.

****

Cami savored her glass of wine, taking in the vibrant nightlife of Atlanta. From the VIP section, she watched her employees dance under the pulsating lights, swaying to the infectious

Latin beats. Suddenly, her attention was drawn to Felix, who swiftly left the dance floor and hurried outside. Moments later, he appeared in the VIP section, urgency etched on his face.

"Cami, let's go. There's an emergency," Felix exclaimed, prompting Cami to leap to her feet, her thoughts instantly on her children's safety. "Emergency? Are my children okay?" she inquired anxiously, her mind racing to Gabriella and Rowen, home alone.

"Felix, is my daughter all right?" Cami pressed, her concern mounting as Felix took her hand firmly. "Yes, I'll explain in the car. Vamos, vamos, the driver is waiting," Felix responded urgently, leading Cami through the crowd to the awaiting vehicle. Cami's heart pounded with dread as she pleaded for answers.

"Felix, please tell me what's happening," she implored, her voice quivering with emotion. Felix urged the driver to hurry while Cami's anxiety intensified. "Felix, tell me what's wrong, tell me right now," she demanded, fear gripping her.

As they sped through the streets, Felix finally spoke, his tone grave. "Cami, Mateo has been attacked. He managed to crawl to your apartment, where Gabriella and Rowen found him outside the door. He's alive, but I don't know the extent of his injuries. There will be police there, so be careful what you say," he explained, his expression reflecting the seriousness of the situation.

Cami's confusion deepened, tears welling in her eyes as she struggled to comprehend. "I don't understand. Why do I need to be careful? Are Gabriella and Rowen okay? Is Mateo alive?" she questioned, her mind flashing back to the loss of her brother years earlier. The familiar look on Felix's face reminded her of the impending and inevitable doom.

Cami was kept in the dark until she received the fateful news. She didn't want to wait until she arrived to find Mateo dead. Begging Felix for answers, she pleaded, "Please, Félix, tell me what's going on. Is Mateo dead? Please, just be straight with me. Don't let me get there and see him like that. What's happening right now?"

Felix grasped Cami's hand and quickly said, "Camille, I'm going to tell you something, and I don't know if Mateo wants you to know this, but I'm making a decision right now so that you understand the gravity of the situation. Mateo is involved in some things, some illegal activities," he blurted out, and Cami's eyes grew wide. She had suspicions about the amount of money coming in from the business, but….. illegal activities?

Felix continued, "He had a meeting with a man tonight that he didn't feel good about. I offered to come, but he declined. There's more than $170,000 in his apartment. I'm guessing that's what they're after, so I can only assume this is what this is about."

Cami couldn't grasp the weight of his words. The alcohol churned in her stomach, and tears started to fall relentlessly from her eyes. All of her questions replayed in her mind, and everything started to make sense. Cami's hands started to shake as she placed them over her mouth.

Félix stared at Cami, waiting for her response. "Camille, are you okay? I'll let Mateo explain further if he can. Please, do not say anything to the police."

Cami's ears started to ring, Felix's voice sounding garbled. She rubbed the back of her neck, trying to grapple with the sudden information. "Illegal activities, $170,000 dollars… What does all this mean?" she thought, her mind racing as they pulled into the parking space.

Felix and Camille jumped out of the car and ran to the apartment building, where police, fire trucks, investigators, and a swarm of people filled the parking lot. Camille ran through the crowd of tenants and found Gabriella crying, breaking away from Julia's arms.

At the sight of her mother, Gabriella screamed, "Mama, Mama! Mateo has been attacked. I'm trying to talk to him, but he won't respond. He's covered in blood, and I didn't know what to do." Cami quickly assessed Gabriella's condition, ensuring she and her friend Rowen were physically okay despite being in shock.

Cami rushed into the apartment and found Mateo lying on the floor, with paramedics attending to his injuries. His eyes were swollen shut, a gash marked his eye, and blood streamed down his face.

Cami dropped to the floor, crying hysterically, "Mateo, sweetheart, you're going to be okay. Please, go to the hospital. I'll go with you and make sure everything is okay." Mateo, unable to respond verbally, weakly lifted his bloody hand and placed it on Cami's cheek.

Nodding to the paramedics, Cami watched as they carefully lifted Mateo onto a stretcher, where he spent weeks recovering from his injuries. Cami, meanwhile, spent weeks grappling with the shock of Mateo's, her lover's true nature, but she remained dedicated to nursing him back to health, both of them deeply traumatized by the experience.

In a desperate attempt to protect herself legally and keep her children safe, Cami reluctantly ended her relationship with Mateo, only to rekindle it months later, unable to resist his intoxicating pull.

Chapter 2

7:30 AM

Present Day

His body, a blurred vision, approached slowly. She could see him come to focus, a bare body silhouette walking closer and closer as he reached the steamed shower door. She could feel her lips start to swell; she grabbed herself and began to move her fingers back and forth while the water spilled over her body. The door slowly opened, the steam covering his face as the water turned to blood.

Cami's eyes opened with urgency. Realizing that it was only a horrible nightmare, she sighed and propped herself up on her elbows, lifting her sleep mask above her eyes. Aroused and terrified by her dream, she turned to glance at her latest lover, nestled cozily amidst her luxurious silk sheets. With a heavy heart, she laid back down. She was shaken by the memory of her dream about Mateo and that fateful night years earlier, yet relieved it was no longer her reality. Quietly, Cami rose from the bed, wrapping herself in a silk robe. Her gaze fell upon the used condom on the floor, and she grimaced at the thought of the previous night's actions.

Leisurely walking to the wet bar across the room, Cami prepared herself breakfast: a concoction of vodka, clamato juice, a celery stick, and two olives. She stirred the mix with a spoon, glanced at the clock, and then stepped onto the balcony. The sounds of her suitor stirring in the condo reached her ears. The man, slender and well-built, with middle-aged grace, slowly opened the balcony doors, greeting her with a

"Good Morning." Cami, stone-faced, continued to stare at the ocean, sipping her bloody Mary, silently wishing for him to leave.

The man stood there a moment longer, his tight tan body and fitted black pants outlining his form, a white shirt casually held in his arms. He waited for her acknowledgment.

"So, should I call you?" he ventured. Cami, visibly annoyed, rolled her eyes.

"Don't bother," she stated bluntly.

The sound of his footsteps signaled his departure, and the door shutting behind him was a welcome relief to Cami.

Cami continued her morning ritual, scrolling through Facebook and Instagram, immersing herself in the virtual world as a means to shake off the remnants of her unsettling dream and the awkward departure of her latest fling. Her fingers paused mid-scroll when her phone buzzed with a new message.

'Good Morning. Call me at the office this afternoon. I have some things to go over with you,' read the text from her lawyer, Ashley Strong.

The message, though brief, carried a weight of responsibility Cami wasn't ready to shoulder just yet. She quickly closed the message, trying to push aside the sense of duty gnawing at her.

Knowing she couldn't avoid her professional responsibilities for long, Cami realized it was time to check in with Jackie at the office. The thought of having to explain her laziness filled her with reluctance. She groaned, and taking a deep breath to muster her courage, she dialed the office number. Jackie's voice greeted her almost immediately, a mix of amusement and reproach in her tone. "Well, hello, party girl. I see you're running late this morning," Jackie teased, her words tinged with a knowing edge.

Cami couldn't help but let out a small sigh, caught in the act yet again. "Yeah, I had a late night," she admitted, trying to downplay the situation. "I feel fine, really. I didn't drink that much. Took a swig of pickle juice, had me a glass of water, and went straight to bed," she explained, hoping her words would paint a picture of responsibility rather than indulgence.

Cami snickered as Jackie laughed, stating, "Sure you did, bitch. I saw you and the lover boy hop in the Uber from the bar last night. What was his name, by the way? He was hot."

Cami shook her head, looking at the condom on the floor, trying to remember his name. "You know, Jackie, I'd rather not say," she replied.

There was a brief silence before Jackie responded, "Oh my God, bitch, you don't even know, do you?" Cami quickly retorted, "Of course I do, Don, no, John… maybe."

Cami's frustration grew, and she quickly squashed the conversation. "Who fucking cares? I'll never see him again anyway. What's going on at work?" she asked, eager to change the subject.

Jackie hesitantly switched her tone and then relayed the day's agenda. "Well, the girls are packing up now and heading to their respective shifts. The guys just unloaded a truck full of cleaning products. You have a meeting with the facilities and operations director at the University, and Mateo called."

Cami sat silent, momentarily puzzled. "What do you mean he called?" she asked.

"I mean, the phone rang, I answered, it was Mateo. He called. Exactly what I said," Jackie explained sarcastically.

Cami rolled her eyes. "Okay, smartass, I'm just kind of shocked he called the office," she admitted.

"Why are you shocked? You won't answer any of his calls, Cami. You have him blocked everywhere. You need to try to at least communicate with him so that you two can somehow work this out," Jackie exclaimed, stressing the need for Cami to face the situation with Mateo.

Cami got defensive, and her response was sharp and filled with anger. "I am not working out shit, Jackie. All of his skeletons fell at my feet in Paris. That was the final fucking straw. I don't have time for his shit, his stories, lies, women, and, least of all, his kid. Besides, he is playing house with that bitch now, and that other bitch has practically stolen my company name and our idea. I now have that headache to deal with. I wish I would have let Mateo kill that red-headed bitch that day," Cami said, frustration evident in her tone.

Jackie paused, sensing the intensity of Cami's feelings. She realized that bringing up Mateo's call might have been a mistake. "Look, Cami, I am sorry. I shouldn't have told you, but I thought maybe you should know," Jackie said, trying to navigate the conversation carefully amidst Cami's silence. "He is just so upset. He loves his child, he loves you, and he doesn't want things to be this way. You have children; you know how much you love them," Jackie tried to reason.

Cami, taking a deep breath and bracing her hands on the counter, replied, "Jackie, my children were conceived before I met Mateo. They came with me. I didn't tell him some bullshit story like I don't have fucking ovaries; I can't have kids. This child is 11 months old, with some stranger that he now has living in a home that we own."

"Cami, he didn't lie about the vasectomy. He got it done in Mexico, for Christ's sake. It obviously did not work," Jackie proclaimed, attempting to offer some perspective.

Cami started to laugh bitterly. "You think? There's no telling how many more are out there, just like his father, the one man he said he never wanted to be compared to," she hissed, frustration evident in her voice. "I can't believe I am having this conversation with you, Jackie, and you are finding a way to defend him," Cami said, clearly disgusted.

Jackie, choosing her words carefully, responded, "Look, I'm not defending him. I just think that at some point, you need to face him and this situation."

"Duly noted. I'll be in the office around noon," Cami said sarcastically and quickly hit the end button. She made her way to the shower, dropping her silk robe on the floor and stepping into the warm water. She let the water cascade over her, scrubbing the scent of the man from her body, refusing to let herself cry over something completely out of her control.

8:30 AM

Mateo sat at the kitchen table, sipping his water after his failed attempt to reach Cami at the office. When he heard the word

"Papa," he quickly got up and picked up his 11-month-old son, Victor.

"Papa is here, mijo," Mateo said as he cradled his son and walked him to the kitchen table, starting to bounce him on his knee when Esme appeared from the bedroom, a woman he barely knew and the mother of his child.

"Is he fussy this morning?" she asked in a slightly British accent, leaning against the doorway. "No, I don't think so. I believe he is just hungry," Mateo replied. Esme lovingly walked to Victor, picked him up, and headed towards the kitchen.

Mateo watched her walk away and picked up his phone, finding himself in the same position he had been in years earlier, searching for any trace of Cami on social media. An ad came across his screen for Beauty Clean, and there stood Cami, clad in a tight pencil skirt and a black low-cut shirt that hugged her body, her hair slicked back in a long ponytail that touched the top of her ass.

"God, she is beautiful," he whispered to himself as he studied the picture. His gaze was broken by Esme, a far cry different from Cami, with blonde hair and pale skin, beautiful in her own right but nothing in comparison.

"Who's beautiful?" she asked suspiciously. Mateo placed the phone face down on the table and looked up at Esme. "Oh, no one, just a puppy. I was looking to get Victor," he lied.

Esme turned and walked away, not daring to ask Mateo to see his phone or question his answer further. She had been watching him grieve for months over Cami, giving him no choice but to leave Camille to have a relationship with his son.

Mateo could feel Esme's aggravation at his obvious lie and followed her to the bedroom.

"What is your problem, Esme?" he asked as Esme quickly turned around, Victor on her hip.

"Nothing, do I appear to be angry?" Esme replied with a condescending tone.

Mateo shook his head. "Don't play games with me; the look you gave said it all," he scowled.

"I know you are looking for her again, Mateo. I am not an idiot. I can see it in your face every time you pick up that bloody phone," Esme spat out angrily.

Mateo, with hands planted firmly on his hips and lips pursed in frustration, couldn't hold back the questions he'd been dreading any longer. "Did you know we were in Paris? Did you follow me there? Why didn't you tell me you were pregnant?" he demanded, his voice tense with the need for answers.

Esme laid Victor down in his crib. She then turned to face Mateo, her expression a mix of desperation and sorrow as she tried to explain. "Because I heard what happened to Scarlett in Miami. When she said she was pregnant, and when she told me you had a vasectomy, I didn't think I could get pregnant. And with Fernando being the father of Scarlett's son, I was even more convinced I couldn't. So, when I found out I was pregnant, I knew Victor was yours. You were the only man I had been within those months. I knew it wasn't some immaculate conception, Mateo," Esme yelled, her voice breaking as she started to cry.

"And besides, when I found out, I knew you would never leave her or kill me in the process," Esme added, her voice thick with emotion.

Mateo shook his head in disbelief. "But I did leave her, Esme. You have given me no choice. She is my wife. I am trying to make this work for Victor, but you and I don't know each other. It was a short fling, and sadly, I miss my wife. But I love my son more than anything," Mateo explained, his voice laden with regret and a plea for understanding.

Esme's voice rose, her words fueled by a mix of love and hurt. "It wasn't a fling to me, Mateo. I love you, and Victor was conceived out of love, as far as I am concerned. I am sorry you do not feel the same!" Esme screamed.

As Victor began to cry, Esme stormed off to the bathroom, slamming the door behind her and sobbing hysterically. Mateo, frustrated and concerned, picked up his son. He tapped on the bathroom door, knowing he needed to smooth things over with Esme to avoid being away from Victor.

"Esme? Can you hear me? Listen, I am sorry. I am new to this. Forgive me, please. I need to meet my uncle. Can you please come out and get Victor? I will call the nanny to come and help you today," Mateo begged.

Esme eventually opened the door and took Victor into her arms. "Thank you," Mateo said softly, kissing her on the forehead before heading to the shower.

Overwhelmed with nausea at the thought of a future with Esme. He could not bare the thought of spending the rest of his life with this whining bitch. Mateo realized he needed to find a way back to Cami.

Chapter 3

10:45 AM

Cami entered the office sporting her oversized, impenetrable sunglasses, bypassing Jackie in a b-line directly to her desk. Jackie's gaze followed, sensing her friend's despair yet hesitant to confront her moodiness. After some contemplation, though, she decided to reach out once more.

Opening the door, Jackie asked, "Are you going to hide behind your sunglasses all day?" She watched as Cami sifted through her desk drawer.

"Yes, I just might," Cami replied, "the light is bothering me, and I have a splitting headache." Jackie looked at her, puzzled,

"But I thought you said you felt fine after drinking some pickle juice," Jackie said with skepticism.

"That was two hours ago. Now, I've got a headache," Cami replied, avoiding Jackie's gaze.

Jackie moved closer to Cami's desk, gently pulling her hand away from the drawer.

"Stop, let me help," she said, fetching a box of goodie powders and handing one to Cami. Swiftly, Cami downed the powder and washed it down with water from her pristine water bottle.

"Oh my God, thank you," she sighed, collapsing into her desk chair with a sense of relief.

Jackie folded her arms, a look of disapproval etched on her face. "You know those things will eat a hole in your stomach if you keep downing them like that?" she warned.

Cami leaned her head back, tossing her sunglasses onto the desk and rubbing her eyes. "Good, maybe they will eat the rest of my organs," she responded with a hint of dark humor.

"Preferably my heart first," she added. The tension broke as both women started to laugh.

The laughter faded when Jackie leaned down and embraced Cami. "I am going to miss you," she said lovingly. Cami quickly pulled away, refusing to dwell on Jackie's resignation that had been turned in two weeks earlier and, more importantly, refusing to cry.

"I know; I am going to miss you too. Do you have anyone lined up to take your place?" Cami asked, her tone blunt.

"Damn, don't get so emotional, Cam," Jackie frowned, her voice dripping with sarcasm, as they navigated this moment of transition with a mix of humor and unspoken emotions.

Cami softened her tone, "I'm sorry, I just don't have time to be emotional right now. So, did you find me someone or not?" she asked with frank curiosity.

Jackie tilted her head, her expression one of compassion as she drew in a breath. Behind Cami's stern facade, Jackie could sense the sadness. "Yes, I did, as a matter of fact. I'm not sure if you'll love her or hate her, but she's pretty awesome. A real go-getter and beautiful, too. She'll fit right in at Beauty Clean," Jackie said with a hint of excitement.

"Great. What's her name?" Cami asked, her interest seeming to wane at Jackie's assessment of the woman.

Jackie squinted her eyes slightly, trying to read Cami's mood, "Well, her name is Luna," she revealed.

Cami tilted her head, a hint of curiosity breaking through her disinterest, "Luna? Like the moon? Is she your cousin or something?" Cami couldn't help but smirk.

"Yes, like the moon. And no, she's not related. She's a bit out there, but I think she'll be perfect," Jackie assured her, optimism coloring her tone.

Cami eyed Jackie with a blend of skepticism and disbelief. "Jesus, Jackie, what are you getting at with 'Out there'?" she demanded. "Is she going to fuck one of my boyfriends? Is she crazy or something? I swear, I can't deal with any more madness around here," Cami vented.

"Calm down, Cami. She's not crazy; she's just, let's say, passionate," Jackie reassured, rolling her eyes at Cami.

Cami shook her head, exhausted. "So, my assistant is now going to be Luna, and she might be a lunatic. Great, thanks!" Despite the tension, they both managed a light laugh.

Then, Jackie grabbed Cami's hand, and Cami could sense a shift in the conversation. She looked at Jackie with a small frown. "I have some news. I've been hesitant to share, given everything, but I want to tell you more than anyone," Jackie said, her excitement barely contained.

Cami looked at her friend, silent, waiting for the news she was about to receive. Cami nodded, and as if that was the cue Jackie had been waiting for, she exclaimed, "I'm pregnant, Cam!"

Cami's eyes sparkled with joy as she wrapped her arms around her friend in a warm embrace. "Am I really going to be an auntie?" she exclaimed, barely containing her excitement.

Jackie nodded, her eyes brimming with tears, "Yes, yes, yes! Marcelino is over the moon. Actually, this is why I've decided to resign. I kept it under wraps initially because I wanted to ensure everything was okay. But now, I'm ready to be a mom and raise my child at home.

Cami offered her friend a tender, supportive smile. "You're going to be an incredible mom. And guess what? I'm going to organize the most amazing baby reveal and shower for you!" she announced, and Jackie's face lit up with anticipation.

"Marcelino is hoping for a girl, but honestly, I just want our baby to be healthy," Jackie shared, her voice thick with emotion.

Cami hugged her friend once more, reassuring her, "No matter what, he or she will be absolutely perfect."

Their bubble of excitement was momentarily popped by the sound of a phone ringing. It was Anthony, Cami's youngest son, calling.

"Hi, baby," Cami answered right away.

"Hi, Mama. What do you have planned for today?" he inquired.

"Nothing that can't wait. What's going on?" Cami replied, her attention now divided as she heard whispers in the background.

"Michael, Gabriella, and I wanted to take you to lunch. Are you free?"

Cami found the conversation odd and sensed her children were up to something, but she didn't let on about her suspicions.

"Absolutely. Where would you like to go? No Mexican or Cuban, by the way," Cami said.

Anthony giggled at his mother's sarcasm. "Of course not. We were thinking about the trusty Italian, maybe Mona's Pizza Place?"

Cami smiled. "Sounds good. See you there around 1:00 or so?" she offered.

"Okay, love you," Anthony said before disconnecting. Cami hung up the phone and turned to Jackie.

"This is what you get to look forward to for the next 20 chapters of life: your kids planning an attack that appears heartfelt," Cami said knowingly.

"If my children are half as wonderful as yours, I know I've done something right," Jackie replied.

The two women shared a halfhearted smile and hugged, aware that the crossroads of friendship were upon them.

1:00 PM

Cami pulled into Mona's Pizza place and noticed her three beautiful children sitting on the patio at a large wrought iron table, laughing and chatting with each other. She paused to watch them, filled with pride. They were all successful, all beautiful, and all hers.

Taking a deep breath, she prepared herself for the lively conversation ahead, knowing she should cherish this moment of tranquility before joining her three very opinionated children. Gabriella spotted her mother and waved her over with a warm smile.

As Cami entered, the hostess escorted her through the doors to the patio. Michael, Anthony, and Gabriella stood up as their mother was seated. "Can I get you anything, Mrs. Vega?" the waitress inquired.

Cami gave the waitress a look of slight annoyance. "It's Ms. Leone, please. And yes, I would like a Bloody Mary, a double shot of vodka, extra celery, extra olives, light on the pepper, and a splash of Tabasco. Tajín on the rim, oh, and please use Clamato juice," she specified. After completing her order, Cami leaned back in her chair and smiled, catching her children's puzzled glances.

Anthony was the first to break the silence, his tone a mix of amusement and disbelief. "I mean, wow, Mom, it's mid-afternoon. We thought maybe beer or wine, but you're going straight for the vodka?"

"It's her liquor lunch, Anthony. Don't act shocked," Gabriella chimed in, reminding her brother of their mother's penchant for indulgence, while Michael couldn't resist adding his own jab, "Especially don't forget the booze breakfast," he quipped with a hint of sarcasm. Cami's patience wore thin at the veiled insults.

"Jesus, you all invite me here. I order one drink, and while you three sip on your beverages of choice, I'm suddenly the one with a drinking problem?" she retorted, her frustration evident.

Anthony, sensing the tension, reached for his mom's hand. "Calm down, Ma. We're just joking. Don't get so defensive. And for the record, I'm drinking Coke. I'm not old enough for a liquor lunch," he pointed out with a gentle smile. Michael and Gabriella couldn't help but laugh, easing the atmosphere just as the waitress returned with Cami's Bloody Mary.

Cami took a quick sip to verify its quality. "Thank you, it's perfect," she said, visibly relaxing. With the initial tension wearing off, she leaned back, enjoying her drink, and dived into the conversation she knew was inevitable. "So, what's this about? I know it's not a lunch date without an agenda."

Gabriella gazed at her mother with eyes full of compassion and gently said, "Of course it is, Mom. We just wanted to check on you to make sure you're okay. We did tease you a bit about your particular request for a Bloody Mary, but, in all honesty, we're concerned about your drinking as well."

Cami, with a hint of defiance, rolled her eyes and took a large gulp of her drink, trying to retort before she accidentally swallowed a whole olive, causing her to cough abruptly. Michael, quick to react, began patting her on the back. "Mom, are you okay?" he asked with concern.

After a brief struggle, Cami managed to swallow the olive and placed her hands on her chest, reassuring her children, "Yes, I'm fine. And I don't have a drinking problem. The only issue is I drink them too fast," she quipped, patting her chest for emphasis.

Her children couldn't help but laugh at their mother's antics. Yet, Gabriella saw through the humor, recognizing it as her mother's way of skirting around the issue. But she was to address the elephant in the room; she decided to call her out on it.

"Mom, you're funny, but we can't just ignore that you've been through a lot recently. We're all worried about you, and..." Gabriella trailed off, exchanging glances with her brothers, fully aware that this confrontation might push Cami to her limits.

Cami, sensing the gravity of Gabriella's pause, looked at her daughter with a mixture of anticipation and apprehension. "And what?" Cami pressed, her voice tinged with a challenge.

All three children sat in silence when Gabriella, after a brief debate with herself, finished her sentence, "Mateo called us." Cami shook her head in disbelief, but as Gabriella's words set in, she turned to stare away from her children, fighting back tears. They could see she was trying too hard to compose herself but didn't say anything and waited for her to respond.

Cami, feeling somewhat in control, asked the inevitable question, "Why?"

"Well, Mom, he got all of us on a conference call," Gabriella continued, "trying to explain himself and what happened. And honestly, Mom, I feel bad for him," she said, her voice filled with compassion as she nodded towards Michael to speak.

"We do too, Mom, and so does Nonna," Michael added.

Cami's eyes widened as her voice rose, "He actually put you three on a conference call to explain himself? And somehow his manipulative, narcissistic, gaslighting explanation has all three of you feeling sorry for him?"

Michael could see his mother's frustration interrupting her outburst, "Mom, please hear us out on this. If you don't listen to him, listen to what he has said to us," Michael pleaded.

Cami let out a loud sigh and rubbed her temple, clearly exhausted by the exchange. Closing her eyes for a brief moment, she reached into her bag and pulled a cigarette from her cigarette tin. Her children watched her as she lit it up. They did not approve of her indulgence but decided to keep their opinion to themselves..... for now.

Cami took a long drag of the cigarette, staring at the smoke and waiting to hear what Mateo could have possibly said to her children to convince them that what he did was okay.

"Go ahead. I can't wait to hear this," she said to her children, followed by a dry chuckle.

Chapter 4

1:05 PM

North Miami

Mateo and Aldo strolled around their latest neighborhood development, marveling at the Green project that had caught the attention of the local news.

"You never cease to amaze me, Mateo. The way you've marketed this neighborhood has really taken off," Aldo said in awe, impressed by Mateo's vision.

"It's the wave of the future, Tio. Smaller homes, solar panels, and within walking distance of the city cut down on emissions, and the homes are affordable. It's really common sense if you ask me," said Mateo.

"Common sense? Is that what you call it?" Aldo chuckled.

Mateo looked at his uncle with suspicion. "Yes, Aldo, that's exactly what I call it. What are you getting at?"

"I wish you applied that same common sense when it comes to women. Maybe then you wouldn't be dealing with this very lack of common-sense situation," Aldo remarked in a condescending tone.

Mateo took offense and snapped back, "Don't start this, Tio. I could have never seen this coming. I took every precaution not to have children, and evidently, that was not in God's plan for me. The only common sense I lost was thinking that a vasectomy in Mexico was a good idea. How could I have known after all these years?

"No, Mateo. Cheating on Cami is what got you here, not your failed vasectomy," Aldo reminded him.

Mateo dropped his head in regret, feeling a pang in his chest at the mention of Cami's name. "I am going to win her back, Tio. One way or another, I will win her back," Mateo stated with determination.

"I think that game show is over, Mateo. Have you heard about her latest shenanigans? She has got every man in Miami begging for her attention, and as painful as it is to tell you, she has entertained a few," Aldo stated regretfully.

Turning away as if to shield himself from the truth, Mateo seemed to hope that by not facing Aldo, he could somehow escape his words. Aldo placed his hand on Mateo's shoulder. "I know it hurts, but you need to let her be. Give her the business, let her franchise the name, and give her the royalties. She deserves at least that much. She's been through enough, learning of this child, and now Scarlett is trying to steal the business name and opening a Beauty Clean in Paris. It's a lot. All her troubles have been because of your indiscretions with other women. I know you don't want to hear this, but sadly, it's the truth," Aldo stated.

Mateo scowled, turning to his uncle. "Don't you think I fucking know that, Tio? I've heard about the men. She's acting out; she's hurt. I get it; it's all my fault, but she is mine, and that will not change," Mateo said sadly.

Aldo looked at Mateo with discretion. "Trust me on this, Mateo, let Beauty Clean and Cami go. The sooner, the better. Move on with Esme and raise your son. Listen to me, just this once."

Aldo walked away, leaving Mateo with his thoughts. Mateo stared at Aldo as he drove away, trying to understand the urgency in his words. He knew his uncle all too well and felt something was amiss.

One Week Later

A week had passed since Jackie broke the news of her pregnancy, leaving Cami on edge as she anticipated the arrival of her new assistant.

Entering Beauty Clean, her gaze landed on a tall, middle-aged blonde seated in the lobby. With no sign of Jackie in sight, Cami approached the woman.

"Hi. May I help you?" she asked the strange woman.

The woman quickly stood up, "Hi, I'm Luna, your new assistant. Jackie told me to come in today so she could start training me," she explained.

Cami scanned past Luna, hoping to spot Jackie, then refocused. "Oh, okay. So where is she?" she asked, her tone suspicious.

Luna gestured towards the bathroom. As Cami approached, the sound of loud retching stopped her in her tracks. Knocking on the door, she called out, "Jackie, are you okay?"

Both Cami and Luna cringed as the unmistakable sound of vomit hitting the floor reached their ears.

"Dammit, it's all over the floor," Jackie groaned from within.

Luna, turning to Cami, whispered, "Look, I'm not cleaning that shit up. I don't have to do that, right? That's not in the job description?"

Before Cami could respond, Jackie slowly walked out of the bathroom, looking worse for wear, sweating, and leaning against the door frame. "Cami, I need to go home. This baby feels like a demon inside of me," she said in a ragged voice.

Both Cami and Luna covered their noses with their shirts, grimacing as Cami gestured towards the exit.

Jackie, collecting her belongings, passed Mia, Beauty Clean's most reliable employee, on her way out. Just then, Luna's eyes brightened at the sight of a Beauty Clean maid, hopeful she would take on the daunting task in the bathroom.

"What's wrong with her?" Mia asked, just as Jackie was sick again outside.

"She's pregnant," Cami and Luna replied in unison, their voices blending together in the chaotic moment.

"Good grief. Is it in the water? Like, everybody is popping out babies," Mia commented with disdain. She immediately regretted her words but was relieved when the awkwardness dissolved as both women erupted in laughter.

"What?" Mia asked, confused by her boss's and the new assistant's laughter.

Cami and Luna were laughing uncontrollably, trying to explain that they had just met and Luna's objection to cleaning up the vomit meant the task would inevitably fall to Mia. Mia finally understood the situation.

"Oh no, Cami, do I really have to clean that up? Please, can't one of the male cleaning crew do it? I signed up to work with hot men, not pregnant women," Mia exclaimed, half-joking, half-serious.

Cami and Luna fell back on the lobby couch, laughing uncontrollably. Once Cami was able to speak, she said, "I'll get Ralph to do it. Go on and get your things and head to your appointment," she managed to say through her laughter. Mia quickly ran to the storage closet, grabbed her things, and left before Cami could change her mind.

"Ralph," Cami called out. A cleaning crew staff member hastily walked to the front office. "Yes," he said, getting a whiff of the vomit from the bathroom. His grimaced face made the two women laugh even harder.

Cami rolled around on the couch, trying to catch her breath and give the order for the clean-up. "Oh my God," she said, holding her stomach.

"I haven't laughed this hard in a long time," Cami remarked, tears of laughter rolling down her face, pointing Ralph to the bathroom. "Please clean that up." Ralph hesitantly turned away to retrieve the mop bucket and cleaning materials.

The two women finally gained their composure when Luna looked at Cami. "Well, it's nice to finally meet you." Cami blew out yet another laugh. "Nice to meet you, too. I think you are going to work out just fine."

6:00 PM

Mateo walked into the penthouse, anxiety in his steps as he made his way to Victor, who was bouncing in his chair. "Come here to Papa, little man," he said, picking him up. It was then that a peculiar smell caught his attention—the unmistakable scent of burnt bread.

"What the hell is that smell?" Mateo asked, moving towards the kitchen. There, he found Esme frantically trying to wave smoke away from the smoke alarm. "I tried to make bread pudding, but it didn't turn out the way I wanted it," Esme explained, breathless from the smoke.

Observing the scene, Mateo couldn't help but feel a mix of emotions. He half-smiled, flattered by Esme's attempt, yet his mind wandered to the delicious meals Cami used to prepare.

"It didn't turn out at all, Esme. I've told you to stop trying to cook. I will send you to cooking class if I have to, but you are going to burn the building down," Mateo said, his frustration evident as he handed Victor to Esme and threw the burnt bread pudding in the sink. "Please take him to the other room until this smoke clears," he added with a hint of disdain.

Esme didn't hesitate to follow Mateo's direction and, without a word, took Victor to the bedroom. Mateo stepped outside onto the balcony to escape the smoke, leaning against the railing and shaking his head at his situation. "How the fuck am I going to get out of this?" he pondered aloud. Soon after, Esme joined him, her voice soft and apologetic. "I'm sorry, Mateo. I just wanted to do something special for you."

The sincerity in her voice melted Mateo's frustration, and he opened his arms to hug her. Esme hesitated for a moment before she fell into his embrace, resting her head on his chest.

"I know you did," he said, acknowledging her intentions. Despite his longing for Cami, the physical closeness with Esme stirred a different kind of desire within him. Subtly, he began to caress her back, his hands wandering beneath her dress in a bold gesture, lifting her dress.

"Is our boy asleep?" he asked in a low and seductive whisper.

Esme looked up at him, her eyes reflecting a mix of surprise and anticipation. Her lips parted slightly as she answered him, "Yes, he is."

Mateo started to passionately kiss her as she unzipped his pants. He quickly picked her up, taking her to the couch where he laid her over the back, entering her body, rubbing the base of her back as he slid in and out of her, his thoughts focusing on her, the mother of his child, trying to feel that passion he longed for in Cami.

He found it difficult to let himself go. He fought the thought of Cami as he pushed himself inside of her until he could not fight it anymore. The struggle within him grew; the image of Cami infiltrated his mind, her piercing green eyes and her long black hair draped over her breast becoming almost tangible.

For a brief moment, he allowed himself to believe that Cami was there with him, that the passion they shared was rekindled, and that he was making himself a part of her as he always did when they made love. But reality soon shattered this illusion when he quickly opened his eyes to see the blonde-haired woman beneath him on his couch and under his spell.

Mateo quickly pulled away, his actions a reflection of his inner turmoil. As he caught his breath, sweat dripping from his forehead, the realization of his actions, and the longing for what was lost washed over him. He looked at Esme again, his reality, leaving him to confront the consequences of his choices and the memories of Cami that still haunted him.

Chapter 5

Two Months Later

Cami and Luna's friendship blossomed beautifully over the following months. They were inseparable, or "two peas in a pod," as Annaliese, Cami's mother, often remarked in her charming southern drawl.

Luna quickly caught on to her job duties at Beauty Clean and soon commanded the respect of the female staff. Together, they ran the company like a fine-oiled machine, even amidst the looming legal troubles with Mateo. Their fame grew in the Miami club scene, a fact underscored by Cami's decision to have a new billboard featuring both her and Luna, a move that didn't sit well with Jackie. Jackie had never been given a chance at a billboard spot and was determined to confront Cami about it at her gender reveal later that day.

Cami, typically late and still shaking off the remnants of a hangover from a night out with Luna, hurried to the event. It was a beachside affair, organized thoughtfully by the Beauty Clean staff. In her rush, Cami struggled with a car seat, a wrapped gift in one hand, while wearing sandals and a sundress. She was met by Kali, who rushed to help.

"Bitch, what the fuck took you so long? Hell, I'm thinking by the time Cami gets here, this bitch is going to spit this baby out on the beach," Kali exclaimed, bursting into laughter as she rushed over to lend a hand. Her teasing words broke the tension.

Cami, handing her clutch to Kali, gripped the neatly wrapped box tightly, struggling to drudge her way through the sand. "I know, I know; we went out last night and, of course, tied one on," she panted, her breath labored. Kali, her curiosity piqued, turned to Cami. "We? Is this the new girl you have assisting you?" she inquired.

"Yes, that's her. Didn't I tell you about her? You're going to love her. I'm glad you're in town; I want you to meet her tonight. Is your man with you?" Cami replied, adjusting her hold on the box.

Kali gave her a playful yet surprised look. "Is that really a question, bitch? Fuck no, my man isn't with me, and hell yeah, I want to go out," she shot back with a smirk.

Finally reaching the table, Cami plopped down the present and hugged Kali, still catching her breath from the arduous walk. "Yay, I'm so glad you're here. Where's Jackie? I haven't seen her or barely spoken to her since she left Beauty Clean," Cami asked, looking around.

Kali's face fell into a frown, prompting Cami's concern. "What?" she asked, noticing her friend's expression.

"Well, she's not very happy about your new friend being on the billboard. You never asked her to be on one," Kali explained, her tone indicating the potential upcoming drama.

Cami rolled her eyes and exhaled sharply. "Are you fucking kidding me? I can't deal with this shit. I've got enough happening in my life right now. I'm not staying here if I have to listen to this," she declared, starting to walk back to her car.

Kali, however, quickly grabbed her arm. "Come on, Cami. She's hormonal and as big as a house. It's as hot as nine hells out here. Just let her have her reveal, let her bitch at you a bit, then we can leave. You know you can't just walk out and miss this moment," Kali implored.

Cami, meeting Kali's earnest gaze, realized her friend's desperation to avoid drama. "Okay, okay. I'll let her have her moment. Then I'm out. We've got a VIP spot at Eleven in Miami," she conceded with a hint of pride in her voice.

Kali's eyes sparkled with excitement. "Look at you, fancy bitch! You've finally got your shit together without Mateo and all. I'm impressed," she remarked.

Cami and Kali locked arms and started the drudge through the sand. They found Jackie sitting under a tent with a misting fan blowing on her. As they approached, Jackie caught sight of them.

"Glad you could finally make it, Cam. Thought you'd miss the whole party that YOU organized. My baby and I are about to melt into a pile of caramel chocolate here," she said sarcastically, referencing her child's expected Latin skin complexion.

"I'm sorry, sweetie, it's been a long day," Cami said, leaning in for a warm, two-cheek kiss.

Jackie, attempting to rise from her chair, chuckled in response. "Oh, I'm sure. I've heard about you and your new friend painting the town red—and charming the men, no less."

Cami, choosing not to respond to the teasing, instead steadied her friend, offering a helping hand. "Jesus, Jackie, you're only 28 weeks pregnant. Are you sure it's not twins?" she joked.

Jackie, walking over to the fan, stuck her face in front of the spinning blades. Her voice, slightly distorted, carried a tone of mock exasperation. "No, just one. But this little monster is certainly making its presence known!"

"Let's go, ladies. It's getting late, and I am ready to see what we're having," Jackie said, smiling at her two friends. Then, her gaze steadied on Cami. "I do have a bone to pick with you later; my feelings are hurt."

Cami, initially trying to ignore the comment, decided to confront the situation head-on. "And what is that, Jackie?" she asked, as if unaware.

Jackie put her hands on her hips, her stance defensive. "I want to know why you didn't ask me to be on a billboard. I've helped you build that business since the doors opened," she said, tears welling in her eyes.

Cami felt a sense of guilt, lacking comforting words for her emotional friend. She took Jackie's hands in her own. "I don't know, Jackie. I'm sorry. I guess I just never thought about it. Luna and I just…. got along so well, and the photographer offered it one day, so we did it."

"But look," Cami gently placed her hands on Jackie's face, "I will put you on a billboard when you have the baby. Or hey, we can start a business called 'Baby Clean' and put you on the billboard, cleaning up shitty diapers and baby food all over the walls or something."

Kali, finding the idea both sarcastic and hilarious, couldn't contain her laughter. "Fuck yeah, we should totally do that!" she exclaimed with unrestrained excitement. Jackie, her smile widening, looked earnestly at Cami. "You promise?" she asked. "I promise," Cami replied with a reassuring tone.

Cami then guided Jackie towards Marcelino. "Here's your baby mama," she joked, handing Jackie off to Marcelino, who lovingly took Jackie's hand and gave her a soft kiss.

Everyone gathered around in eager anticipation.

The countdown began. "Three... Two... One..." the crowd shouted. Suddenly, the sound of fireworks filled the air, accompanied by a shower of blue sparkles. "Oh wow, it's a boy," Cami announced, her voice mixing surprise and joy.

As Cami put her arms around Kali, embracing her with happiness for their friend, she started to feel emotional, thinking of Mateo and the son he would never have with her—a gift she could never give him. Shaking her head to dispel these thoughts and quickly wiping away her tears, she grabbed Kali's arm. "Let's get the fuck out of here. I'm ready to party," she said, determined to shift her focus back to the celebration.

8:30 PM

Esme, feeling content with the attention Mateo had shown her earlier, decided it was time to take Victor and leave for the evening. She packed her bag and headed to a friend's house, allowing Mateo a night to himself.

As they prepared to leave, Mateo gave Victor a loving kiss on the forehead and walked Esme to the awaiting driver. He handed the driver a tip and closed the door of the SUV, watching as they drove off. A sense of relief washed over him, appreciating that he was offered a bit of freedom.

Mateo strutted back to his penthouse, his thoughts again drifting to Cami. He had his little 'birds,' as he called them, throughout Miami's nightlife, keeping tabs on Cami's whereabouts, her frequent hangouts, and the people she associated with. For a long time, Mateo had stood back, giving Cami a break from the revelation of his child. But now, his patience had worn thin; he was eager to win her back.

In a state of determination, he got dressed and made a phone call to one of his contacts. "Any word on where she is going tonight?" Mateo asked, expecting a swift and informative response.

"Yeah, I just received a call that she's got a VIP spot at Eleven Nightclub. She'll be there with Kali and Luna, her new assistant," the voice on the other end of the line informed Mateo.

Upon receiving the information that Cami was at the Eleven Nightclub with her friends Kali and Luna, Mateo abruptly ended the call and dropped his phone onto the bed. While adjusting his cufflink, he dabbed on his favorite cologne, feeling relaxed and unrushed, knowing he had to allow Cami time to settle in and possibly get tipsy before he made his move.

However, just as he was about to leave, his phone vibrated on the bed. Seeing Aldo's name on the screen, Mateo sighed in frustration. "How in the hell does this man know what I'm doing? It's like he's in my fucking brain," he muttered to himself before picking up the call.

"Yes, Uncle," he answered, unable to mask his irritation.

"Mateo, I need to talk to you," Aldo said urgently, skipping any formalities.

Mateo's agitation intensified. "About what? I've got plans tonight. Can't it wait?"

"No, Mateo. Can I come over?" Aldo asked, hoping for an invitation.

"No. Can't you just tell me over the phone?" Mateo replied bluntly.

Aldo's voice took on a tone of panic. "Okay, can I meet you somewhere?"

This piqued Mateo's curiosity. "What's so urgent, Aldo?" he inquired again.

"Meet me at the British Rose Café in 30 minutes," Aldo suggested.

Mateo furrowed his brow, puzzled but curious by his uncle's eagerness to talk. Despite his initial plans, he agreed to the meeting. "Okay, I'll see you there."

Chapter 6

9:00 PM

Mateo entered the British Rose Jazz Café, immediately enveloped by a welcoming ambiance of dim lighting and soft jazz music floating through the air. The small bar's mahogany walls gleamed under the subdued light, casting a cozy glow throughout. His eyes caught sight of an antique phonograph tucked away in a corner, and he couldn't help but be transported back to the 1920s, reminiscing about his wedding just over a year ago. His trip down memory lane was abruptly interrupted when his uncle called out,

"Mateo, over here," Aldo called, waving Mateo over to a private corner table in the nearly empty bar. As Mateo pulled out his chair, his eyes roamed, taking in the lack of patrons and starting to question his uncle's choice of venue.

"Aldo, where did you find this place? If I didn't know any better, I'd think some mafioso is going to come out guns blazing. This place is dead. Which is surprising because it has a really nice vibe," Mateo observed, impressed despite his reservations.

Aldo leaned forward, urgency evident in his voice. "Mateo, you need to listen closely. The FBI is on to Beauty Clean. They suspect it's a front for a prostitution ring," he disclosed.

Mateo's heart skipped a beat, and his attention focused on Aldo. "Who told you this? And have you mentioned it to anyone else?" he inquired, anxiety creeping into his voice.

Aldo sat back, taken aback by the question but clear in his response. "Do you think I would tell anyone before you? Hell no. I haven't spoken to anyone. I've been hearing whispers, but it was confirmed today by the Mayor," Aldo stated intently.

"The Mayor?" Mateo asked, shocked at the revelation. "But he's a client of Beauty Clean, along with half the city's officials, not to mention we even have a senator now. And the local celebrities... They all rely on our services," Mateo argued, his mind racing.

"How could this happen? The services offered by the girls are independent of their contracts with Beauty Clean. Cami was adamant about that." The whole thing didn't make any sense to Mateo.

Aldo's voice dropped to a whisper as he leaned back, "I know this, Mateo, but I believe Fernando's wife has sparked the investigation after finding out about Scarlett and their love child. And it's an election year; you know these politicians will do anything to ruin each other and take everyone down with them. Mateo, you must turn this business completely over to Cami, get out of it, and live your life with Esme and Victor. Tell her she can have it, stop whatever it is you have created within this company, get rid of any financial transaction and evidence, and if she must take the heat, let her have it. She will have a better chance of getting out of this than you will. The contracts will save her," Aldo insisted, his voice laced with fervor.

Mateo could feel his blood start to boil, "Have you lost your fucking mind, Aldo? I will never do that to her. She is still my wife, in case you have forgotten, and she knows nothing about any prostitution within Beauty Clean. She has no idea what goes on in these homes or with half the women she has employed. I control that; she controls the legitimacy of the company. That is why I will not let Beauty Clean go completely; I cannot allow her to find out or take the fall for something I encouraged with these clients. Cami is innocent in all this," Mateo retorted angrily.

Aldo slammed his fist on the table, his frustration mirroring Mateo's. "Mateo, she is not your wife; she filed the annulment after you returned from Paris. Your marriage to her is over. Why would you risk everything we have worked for, for her? Give her what she wants and get out of this mess," Aldo pressed with a mix of anger and desperation.

Mateo hung his head, trying to keep his anger in check, the weight of Aldo's words bearing down on him as he tried to comprehend the complexity of his emotions and the difficult decisions ahead.

"The annulment hasn't been finalized; I've contested it," Mateo tried to reason, showing Aldo that there was still hope.

He continued, "She filed on the grounds of fraud. We're supposed to go to court soon, but I'll fight it if I can. Besides, I need to talk to her about this before it goes public. Most of the harlots come from Scarlet's business in Paris. She has no idea I own Beaute Propre in Paris. She saw the sign when we were on our way to the Eiffel Tower, but I brushed it off. It was in French, so I just explained it away as a coincidence.

"I just wanted Scarlett's conniving ass out of Miami, and that was the only way I knew how. Fernando owns 50 percent of the business as an assurance he can see his son. Scarlett hires many of the prostitutes out of the Paris office. The investigation probably started there. I'm sure she learned from Cami and copied the contracts for the girls to sign, to cover her ass." Mateo waved the waiter over and paid for Aldo's drink. Taking a sip of his water, he got up from the table. "Don't say a word about this. I'll deal with the outcome, and I'll speak with Cami," Mateo stated.

He left the bar and headed for the Eleven Nightclub. Aldo shook his head in disbelief and hissed, "Harlots, psst...so that's what you call them. He's going to be the ruin of us all."

****

Cami was excited for Kali and Luna to meet; the two shared a striking resemblance and personality. The three women got dressed at Cami's condo in South Beach. Cami wore a sexy low-cut lapel collar pink blazer dress, barely concealing the edges of her breasts, and her tie-leg design pink high-heel shoes to match. Kali, tall in stature, donned a pink sequined camisole top with a V-neck paired with black leather shorts and heels.

Luna opted for a more conservative look with a black sleeveless zipper tank and black shorts. Despite preferring not to accentuate her height, Luna chose low-heeled sandals that still matched Kali's stature.

When the three women emerged, they burst into laughter, looking at each other dressed in similar colors. "Look at us; we look like the dynamic Beauty Clean trio, all in pink and black. Let's go, ladies. I have arranged a driver downstairs," Kali exclaimed, thrilled to start the night. Cami looked at Luna with a sparkle of mischief in her eyes. "You ready for this?"

Luna responded with a half-concerned smile, "Do I have a choice?"

"Not really," Kali and Cami answered simultaneously, laughing as they walked to the elevator, slipping their favorite lip glosses into their handbags.

9:15 PM

As the girls made their grand entrance into Eleven Nightclub, they walked in side by side, capturing the attention of everyone around. The vibrant beats of Latin music filled the air, setting an exhilarating backdrop for the night. They were quickly escorted to their VIP section of the club, where bottle service and a view of the dance floor awaited them.

"So ladies, a toast, shall we?" Kali raised her glass, "May the roof above us never fall in, and may our friendships never fall out."

Kali tilted her glass toward Luna when Cami chimed in, "I got one, I got one. 'Here's to the men that we love, and here's to the men that love us. But the men that we love aren't the men that love us, so fuck them, and here's to us.'" The girls clinked their glasses.

"I guess it's my turn?" Luna asked.

"Yes, yes, yes, girl, you have to give us one," Kali shouted over the music.

"Ok, ok, here it goes," Luna stated, ready to keep the toasting tradition going. "It's not the length, it's not the size, it's how many times you can make it rise."

Kali and Cami's mouths dropped open before they screamed, "Fuck yeah, bitch, you are one of us!!"

As the three ladies started to dance, their movements drew in a crowd of admirers to their VIP area. Amidst the blur of intoxicating music and the haze of alcohol and substances, Cami's gaze locked onto a striking figure across the room—a young man with the dark allure of Mateo, featuring black hair, deep-set dark eyes, and clad in an elegant red vest suit complemented by black shoes. His arms were covered in tattoos.

As Cami stared at the man, Kali caught sight of where Cami's attention had fallen and leaned in to whisper with a hint of amusement, "Bitch, that looks like the devil himself."

Cami chuckled, keeping her eyes fixed on the man as she moved her body back and forth. "Well, call me Jezebel because he is starting to walk this way, and so are his friends," she said, using her middle finger to motion him to the VIP and pointing at his two friends for an invitation.

Luna noticed the banter between the two and nudged Kali, "Looks like we have a bite, and she is reeling them in."

Kali, not surprised, held her hand up to give a high five to Luna. "That's how we roll, bitch. I've taught her well," Kali stated, laughing and pouring herself another glass of Champagne.

The three men walked into the VIP section and, without a word, chose their respective partners and started swaying against the women's bodies. Cami didn't know if it was instant attraction or if he reminded her so much of Mateo. She placed her arms around his neck, moving her hips back and forth; she could feel his erection when he leaned in, gracing her lips with his tongue, distracting her from everyone around her.

Her eyes shut. The smell of his cologne intensified her desire, her movements becoming more provocative against his thigh, her wetness evident through the fabric of her panties. Planting her face in his neck, tasting his cologne, she slid her tongue back and forth, sinking herself into his body under the iridescent lights.

The man slowly pulled back to look at Cami, "You are incredibly beautiful, Amor," he stated in a heavy accent. He bore such a striking resemblance to Mateo, and the words were so familiar that, for a moment, she thought it was him.

Cami was taken aback. She steadied herself, trying to focus through her blurred vision and racing thoughts. She needed to compose herself, not wanting to break the mood or cause alarm. She looked at the man and whispered in his ear, "I'll be right back."

Her heart racing, she left the VIP section and headed for the door, exclaiming, "Excuse me, excuse me," as she made her way through the crowd. Then she dropped her purse. Bending down to pick it up, she recognized the shoes it lay against. She was frozen. She closed her eyes and wanted to crawl the rest of the way out of the building when the hand she knew all too well was extended to her. She slowly grabbed it, knowing there was nowhere she could run.

Chapter 7

Mateo occupied a discreet corner of the bar, his gaze unwaveringly on his wife. He casually pushed his empty glass towards the bartender, requesting another with the nonchalance of someone deeper into their drinks than just water.

"Sir, if you're not going to buy anything, can you please find somewhere else to stand? I have customers who need real drinks," the bartender remarked with blunt disinterest.

Unfazed, Mateo produced three one-hundred-dollar bills from his wallet. "Is this enough for a glass of water?" he asked, his tone dripping with the same lack of impression the bartender's attitude had left on him.

His importance was quickly recognized by another bartender; the young woman was corrected. "Yes, sir, you can stand there as long as you like," she said, her earlier bravado melting into embarrassment.

Mateo turned to look back at Cami when he noticed her wrapped in a man's arms, kissing him, watching his hands move their way up her dress.

In an odd way, Mateo was turned on by her sexiness, the way she moved. He was channeling, envisioning himself standing there holding her the way the stranger did. He noticed her pull away, pushing her way out of the VIP. He quickly left the bar and started towards the VIP, keeping his eyes fixed on her every move until he was almost face-to-face with her. Before he could lock eyes with her, she dropped her handbag at his feet.

He stood there, fixed in position, and looked down at Cami. She was stiff, her hand resting on her handbag and his shoe. He extended his long arm to her, his hand waiting for hers. She grabbed his hand, and he slowly pulled her up. "Hello, Mi Amor," Mateo's voice was deep as their eyes locked. He noticed Cami trembling, her jaw clenched, her face reddened.

"Hello," was all Cami could muster.

"Would you like a drink?" He asked nonchalantly, his nerves hidden under his tough exterior. "No, Mateo. I would like a cigarette," Cami said with defiance, knowing Mateo's disdain for cigarettes.

She started to walk quickly towards the door, Mateo following close behind. "Amor, stop, please stop, Camille," Mateo begged. "Camille Vega, stop, please. Mi Amor, please."

He continued to beg as he followed her out of the door. Cami stopped against the wall and started digging through her handbag for a cigarette, her hands trembling, fighting back tears when she finally put one to her mouth and lit it, drawing in every bit of smoke that could fill her lungs.

Mateo approached her slowly as if he was creeping up on a wild animal, his hands in his pockets to show his surrender. "Can we talk?"

Cami laid her head against the wall, fighting the urge to throw her arms around him and kiss him. "What are you doing here, Mateo, following me? Don't think I don't know about your little fucking informants all over town. I hope they have told you everything you want to know."

Mateo, taken aback by her awareness of his surveillance but trying to deflect, laughed it off. "Cami, I do not have informants; do I have people that may watch you while you're out? Of course, I do. I know you have been acting out. I just want you safe."

Cami kept her head steady on the wall, rolling it sideways to look Mateo in the eyes. "Acting out? Is that what you call it? I'm not a fucking child, Mateo. I don't need your protection," she stated with disgust.

"Look, Cami, I am not here to argue. I just want to talk to you; we have a lot we need to talk about," Mateo pleaded.

"There is absolutely nothing I have to say to you. Go home to your whore, baby mama drama, and your fucking illegitimate child, and leave me the fuck alone," Cami snapped back, her voice rising as she pushed off from the wall, trying to leave the heavy conversation and her feelings behind.

Mateo thought to let her go, but he knew her words were laced with anger. Cami loved children despite the situation; she would never say things like this, and he knew he had to take some responsibility for her hurt.

Mateo started to jog after her. "Cami, stop," he pleaded.

Cami continued to walk, the tears now flowing like a raging river, when suddenly, Mateo reached out, grabbing her arm to spin her around. She fell into his chest, sobbing uncontrollably, as months of pain and heartache came pouring out. She was melting, losing her edge, and giving in to him once again.

All Mateo could do was hold her in that moment. "Shhh, Amor, please don't cry. Let's take a walk," he said as he lifted her chin. "Do you want to walk with me? We don't have to discuss anything right now," he suggested convincingly.

Cami looked up at him, her makeup running down her face. "No, I don't want to walk. I don't want to let you go. Take me somewhere, hold me, that's all I want," she cried.

Mateo, shocked by the invitation but unable to resist, smiled. "Okay, Amor, wherever you want to go, I'll take you."

Cami and Mateo pulled into a familiar high-rise parking garage two miles from the Eleven Nh laightclub. The short drive felt like hours of silence. Cami, stuck in the car, texted Kali to let her know she had left, too emotionally fatigued to fight or explain to her friends. She wanted to feel good just one more time, even if it meant ruining months of emotional repair. She knew she was fading into a honeymoon phase, aware that all the feelings of betrayal and pain would eventually return—the reality of Esme and Victor, the annulment, and the business. All those things eluded her at this moment. She just wanted to feel him again and not say a word.

Mateo parked the car and rushed around to open the door for Cami. She reluctantly grabbed his hand, stepping out of the car. Looking around, she realized where she was. "Wow, I didn't know you still had this place," she stated with suspicion. It was Mateo's first condo, one that Cami had refused to live in when she first moved to Miami. She had thought Mateo had sold it and bought the penthouse but quickly realized this had been his bachelor pad all along.

Cami stood at the edge of the building, hesitating, feeling Mateo's presence just a step behind her. His advance paused as he sensed her rigidity and the silence that had fallen between them, the warmth of her hand fading away.

"What is it, Amor?" Mateo inquired, his voice laced with concern. Cami was surrounded by a storm of thoughts, her mind teetering on the brink of unleashing words filled with bitterness and blame. His eager anticipation to rekindle what they once had only fueled her disdain further. Mateo sensed her growing resentment.

Trying to calm her, he slowly held out his hand, "Please come with me, Cami. I know what you are thinking. I am so very sorry I have hurt you; I want nothing more than to take back everything I have done, but I can't. I need you right now. My body aches without you," he confessed.

Cami held her words, and her heart softened. She knew the pain he was feeling because she felt the same pain and reluctantly took Mateo's hand. He could see her weakness. Picking her up and cradling her in his arms so she would have no escape, he walked her through the garage into the condo. She laid her head on his chest, closing her eyes, trusting him to take her to a safe place.

Mateo lightly set Cami on her feet as they reached the condo, cradling her face in his hands and lightly kissing her lips. He unlocked the door and flicked on the light. The two walked into the condo towards the bedroom. The smell of the condo brought Cami a nostalgic feeling of familiarity. It felt like home, yet somewhere far away from her new reality. Cami slowly walked into the bedroom, where pictures of herself hung on the wall and sat neatly in frames on the dresser.

Cami's growing resentment bubbled to the surface as she stared at the life-size portrait of herself with Mateo that adorned their wall. With a tone laced with disgust, she couldn't help but confront him, "What do all of your whores think, seeing me on the wall while you're with them?" she said with disgust. Mateo, visibly distressed, pleaded, "Please, amor, not now."

But Cami's attention remained anchored to the picture, her thoughts spiraling. "Was it here that your child was conceived? The one you claim couldn't exist because of your supposed vasectomy? How many more secrets are you keeping?" she demanded, her voice a mix of disbelief and sorrow.

Mateo walked behind Cami, placing his chin on her shoulder, "Stop it, please. I know you're angry. I honestly had no idea I could have children. I was just as shocked."

Cami could feel her stomach turn. The thought of a woman giving the man she loved something she could not erupted a wave of emotion that made her feel queasy; the lump in her throat grew larger. She cleared her throat and took a deep breath. Her conscience spoke to her. The voice in her head whispered to her over and over, "Leave, Camille." Mateo could feel Cami's elusiveness; he knew she was ready to run.

Despite the tension, Mateo knew he had to keep her close to share the revelations Aldo had confided in him about the scandal involving Beauty Clean. He had to tactfully inform Cami about the prostitution allegations and the secret dealings in Paris, intended to silence Scarlett after the birth of Fernando's child, whose brother was now running for Mayor in Miami. The allegations would throw Cami into a tailspin. His first order of business was to make love to her, soften her emotions, and gently tell her before it became public.

Mateo placed both of his hands around Cami's small waist. His touch took Cami's breath away; he had not touched her in months. Mateo began slowly kissing her neck. Cami closed her eyes, feeling all the emotions she had been longing for. She could feel herself pulsate, her lips becoming plump with every touch of his hand. She melted into him.

Mateo began to run his fingers through her silky black hair, touching every inch of her body. "I feel like I have been in the desert without a drink of water. I thirst for you, Mi Amor."

As he lifted her in his arms, her legs instinctively wrapped around him, their bodies syncing in a dance as old as time. They passionately kissed for what seemed like hours before he slowly carried her to the bedroom.

Mateo made love to her for hours, in every position, taking in every inch of her body. Sweat poured from both of their bodies. Unaffected by the damp sheets, they continued until they fell asleep in each other's arms, exhausted by the emotions of the moment.

9:30 AM

The sun was shining brightly through the windows, making it hard for Cami to open her eyes due to the glare. She propped herself up on both elbows, noticing that Mateo was not in bed but was enticed by the smell of coffee brewing, her favorite morning drink. It was a welcome change from the morning Bloody Marys she had recently become accustomed to.

Cami got out of bed, slipped into Mateo's dress shirt, and hesitantly walked to the kitchen. She could hear the TV in the background mentioning Beauty Clean, but she suspected it was just a commercial and paid no attention to it. When Mateo saw Cami emerge from the doorway, he quickly turned off the TV. He walked slowly towards her, handing her the morning coffee he knew she would love.

"Buenos Días, Mi Amor," he said in a sexy low tone. Cami remained silent, thinking of ways to undo the damage from months of being apart.

"Are you ok?" Mateo asked softly.

Cami nestled herself on the white leather couch, sipping her coffee. "Not really, Mateo," she began, starting to look around for her purse to retrieve her phone. "Have you seen my purse? I need my phone. I'm sure I have a million calls by now."

Mateo sat down next to Cami and gently placed his hand on her leg, dropping his head in shame and drawing in a deep breath. "I will give you your phone and purse, but Cami, we need to have a discussion. I need to tell you something I have just learned in the past 24 hours. But understand, I am going to take care of this, and you will be fine."

Cami looked at Mateo inquisitively, her heart starting to race. She could not fathom what could be so pressing after all that had happened. "What do you mean, 'I will be fine'?"

She sat back in the corner of the couch, her arms wrapped around her raised legs, staring at Mateo, waiting for him to make eye contact. He rested his elbows on his knees and started to rub his face. "What is it, Mateo? You're making me nervous!"

Mateo lifted his head and turned to Cami. "Camille, Beauty Clean is being investigated," he stated.

Cami remained silent, confused by the revelation. Her gaze locked on Mateo, trying to process the sudden news. "Investigated for what?" she asked, somewhat unaffected.

"Cami, listen to me, investigated for possible prostitution. But it's more like affluent men paying for sex to willing participants, mainly our employees, under the disguise of cleaning, and the FBI is investigating," Mateo stuttered.

Cami quickly stood up and walked around in circles with her hands gripped tightly to her hair. "That's a fucking prostitution ring, Mateo. Are you fucking kidding me right now? What does that mean for me? Am I going to be arrested?" Cami screamed.

"Cami, please calm down. It's election year, and Fernando's wife created this mess after she found out about their love child. That's why Scarlett tried to pin the baby on me. But be assured, I have made some phone calls this morning, and Gabriella is at the office now, destroying some of the paperwork that I have locked away," Mateo explained.

Cami's reaction was immediate and intense, her eyes widening in shock and disbelief. "You have involved my fucking daughter. Oh my God, Mateo, what have you done? I can't fucking believe this."

Cami started to frantically look for her belongings. "I need my phone, and I need to call a lawyer. Jesus, I can't believe you have got me into this. What about the waivers and contracts I made them sign? I worked all this out with the lawyers to protect myself. You mean to tell me the women I have employed are fucking the clients for money and scheduling this shit through my business, and I did not know?" Cami said, her words spilling out in a frantic clutter.

Mateo, in a desperate attempt to handle the situation, grabbed Cami by the arms, trying to calm her down. "Cami, calm down. If anything happens, I will take the fall. I've spoken to our attorneys, and so many affluent people are involved it will be swept under the rug in no time. The business may suffer, but it will come back once we have proven that you took all the necessary precautions to avoid this."

Cami's eyes began to fill with tears, repeating Mateo's words, "The business will suffer? Affluent? Gabriella, my child, is destroying evidence. What the fuck is happening?" Sitting down on the couch, she glared at Mateo, her thoughts racing. Then, she calmly stated, "Call my daughter right now, tell her to leave Beauty Clean and go home. She will not touch another piece of paper or computer in that office!"

Mateo stood frozen, looking at the woman he loved, knowing this would be the final blow. When Cami started to scream, "Do it right fucking now, Mateo!" This jolted Mateo into action. No longer paralyzed, he methodically pulled his phone from his pocket, the weight of the situation heavy in his hands as he dialed Gabriella, preparing to convey Cami's urgent directive.

Mateo was concerned about Cami's reaction to the unfolding situation. He expected her to be upset, but the intensity of her rage took him by surprise.

"Gabriella, I am with your mother. She knows. She wants you to leave the office and go home," Mateo's request was met with pushback from Gabriella.

Cami grabbed the phone, "Gabriella, get the fuck out of that office right now and go home. This is none of your concern."

Cami's frustration overwhelmed her when she threw the phone across the room, shattering a picture of her and Mateo that sat neatly on the counter. She stared at Mateo and the shards of glass that rained down on the floor. It was yet another symbol of her relationship, her business, her marriage, and her life in Miami—shattered glass, never repairable. There was nothing she could do at this point but leave and never look back.

Chapter 8

Three Months Later

Cami sat in the courtroom, her conservative crème-colored suit blending in with the solemnity of the setting, her long black silky hair draped over the back of the chair. Mateo was by her side, his presence a silent testament to their shared history.

As the judge entered the courtroom, Mateo placed his hand over hers in a gesture of support. Cami, however, slid his hand back to its rightful place, a single tear rolling down her face.

Mateo leaned in, his voice low and comforting, "It's going to be ok, Mi Amor."

Yet, Cami remained silent. Her refusal to acknowledge him spoke volumes. Three months had passed, and it was the first time she had seen Mateo since their rendezvous in the condo. She refused meetings with him and would only see their attorney separately.

Her attorney, Ashley Strong, was the best in Miami and represented Cami and Mateo on business matters, but this was much more serious. As Ashley prepared her paperwork, the judge made his way to the bench. The judge looked directly at Cami and Mateo. Camille recognized him from a business event that Mateo and Aldo had hosted two years before. Cami showed no emotion, not knowing if the familiarity of the judge was a good sign or bad.

Ashley looked at Cami with a determined look, "You will be ok either way, Camille."

Cami silently shook her head and rested her hands in her lap as she heard the courtroom doors open and the faint cries of a child. Instantly, Cami knew it was Esme and Victor. She had seen Victor once, refusing to look at pictures or acknowledge his existence after Paris. Her head hung low in response.

Mateo, sensing the overwhelming tension, turned to his uncle and motioned for him to escort Esme and Victor out of the courtroom. He then looked at Cami with a regretful expression, "I'm so sorry, Camille. Aldo has made her leave. I did not know she would show up here." Cami drew in a deep breath, continuing her silence.

The judge shuffled papers around the bench before slamming his gavel, commanding silence in the courtroom. Without delay, he began reading the charges. "In the case against Camille Leone vs. the state of Florida, in regards to count one of solicitation of prostitution and one count of pandering, the state has found that there is not sufficient evidence in this case for an indictment. As for Mateo Vega, in regard to count one of pandering, the state has found that there is not sufficient evidence for an indictment. You are free to go."

The judge swiftly stood up and exited the courtroom. Camille, shocked by the quick and sudden decision, sat in disbelief as she turned to Ashley with questioning eyes. "Is that it? Is this over? I can go?"

Ashley smiled, hugging Camille, and then leaned in to shake Mateo's hand. "That's it, you're free to go. But Cami, can I see you at my office this afternoon?" Ashley asked with an insistent tone.

"Yes, absolutely, whatever I need to do. I'll be there," Cami responded, her voice breathless, relieved that it was all over, her life no longer hanging in the balance. She slowly slung her small handbag over her shoulder and turned to walk away when Mateo stopped her. "Please, Camille, can we talk?"

Cami snatched her arm away with fervor. "Do not ever touch me again. I mean it, Mateo. Do not breathe my name or come within feet of me. You have almost destroyed my entire fucking life, taken me away from my family and my children, and I will never forgive you. Now go live your life with that fucking street whore and little bastard you have."

Cami marched out of the courtroom doors, only to come face-to-face with Esme and Victor. She stood and stared at them both, heartbroken at her loss but also distraught at the disdain she felt for such a beautiful child. Her eyes filled with tears, and she was frozen at the sight of them.

As she could hear Mateo's steps behind her and smell his cologne getting closer, the thought of him nearing her broke her gaze from Esme, and she turned and quickly walked away.

One Month Later

Cami stood in her penthouse, staring at the boxes she had packed. Her hair slicked back in a tight ponytail and a comfortable flowing dress for her flight to Atlanta. She and her family had come to terms with the fact that they all needed to leave Miami and get back to their place of safety in Georgia, where their roots were.

The news of Beauty Clean swept through Miami like a hurricane, and the business was swiftly shut down. Cami knew she had to leave Miami to escape the suffocating grip Mateo had over her and the ever-present cloud of suspicion she lived under with the Miami elite.

After months of silence and relentless begging for her forgiveness, Mateo realized it was of no use; Cami remained dead silent. Resigned to losing her, he settled in with Esme and his son Victor, but not without vowing to himself that he would one day win Camille back. Whispers and rumors of more children floated around, though they were never substantiated. This only reinforced Cami's resolve—she knew she could not live her life like Maria, Mateo's mother, trapped in a cycle she desperately wanted to break free from.

Ashley Strong, Cami's attorney, had been visibly frustrated with Cami after the court proceedings, particularly over Cami's refusal to claim her fair share from Mateo. Nevertheless, the annulment was finalized on the day Cami was set to depart for Atlanta. Cami walked away without claiming anything from Mateo, returning to Georgia with nothing but her initial investments and the remnants of her dignity. The pain of losing Mateo was not as devastating as it was the first time; too much had happened to turn back. The relationship was a broken mess, just like the picture she had seen crash to the floor the last time she saw him.

Cami, saddened by her departure from Miami, wistfully walked through the airport with just a carry-on, as the rest of her life, tightly packed away in the back of a moving truck to a modest A-frame home situated on the outskirts of Atlanta. The tightness in her chest was unbearable as her heart ached, but as she handed her ticket to the agent and slowly walked down the aisle of the plane, taking her seat in business class, a sense of relief washed over her.

She was leaving Mateo behind, allowing him to be with his son and Esme. Miami, with all its chaos and memories, would soon become a distant chapter in her life.

Two Hours Later

The bustling Hartsfield in Atlanta enveloped Cami as she maneuvered her small bag through the airport, the familiar feeling of her Georgia home enveloping her. She looked around at the diversity of people, the large pictures that hung on the wall of musicians that Atlanta had born and bred, and the black and white pictures of the superstructures and city lights.

Engrossed, Cami stood still on the moving sidewalk, letting the art pass by her gaze. This trance was abruptly interrupted when she stumbled off the end, losing her balance and tripping over her rolling bag.

Lying there for a moment, Cami felt a flush of embarrassment wash over her, hesitant to move. Then, a deep voice broke through her thoughts, accompanied by a light chuckle, "Hey lady, are you ok? Are you hurt?"

Without looking up, and her face still pressed against her rolling bag, Cami replied, "Only my pride. Is everyone looking?" Her voice was low, tinged with embarrassment.

The man's laughter offered a moment of relief. "If your ass doesn't get up, they will start looking. There's a shit ton of people about to roll off the end of this thing." He extended a hand towards her. Grasping it, Cami managed to get back on her feet, brushing the hair away from her face only to lock eyes with a familiar figure, Beau Machado.

Her heart skipped a beat, racing uncontrollably as she hung her head, hoping against hope he hadn't recognized her. "Cami?" Beau's voice, filled with surprise, confirmed her fears.

Keeping her head bowed, Cami clutched the handle of her rolling bag, attempting to make a swift departure with a polite "Thank you," accompanied by a nod. But Beau wasn't ready to let the moment pass so easily.

His hand gently caught her arm, prompting a pause. "Cami, is that really you?"

Cami paused, then slowly turned back to face Beau, confirming with a quiet, "Hi, yes, it's me."

Beau's response came with a smile, "Have you been drinking, or are you just clumsy in your older age?"

Cami shot him a look of disgust. "No, Beau, I have not been drinking, and I am not that old. I just tripped, that's all." She began rummaging in her purse, perhaps seeking a distraction from the conversation that was quickly becoming too focused for her comfort.

"You know I am kidding with you; I haven't seen you in so long," Beau tried to lighten the mood, but their exchange was momentarily interrupted by passengers coming off the moving sidewalk. Together, they reached for her rolling bag to move it aside.

"I got it," Cami said, a hint of nervousness in her voice as they sidestepped the incoming rush of people.

"So, what are you doing here? Your Latin lover lurking about?" Beau joked, though the humor faded quickly as he caught the pained expression on Cami's face.

Lowering her head in a mix of sadness and embarrassment, Cami confessed, "No, Beau, we are no longer together. I am moving back to Atlanta."

Beau stood there with a smile, his nod almost saying, "I told you so." It was a mix of vindication and compassion he felt for Cami. "I'm sorry to hear that, I really am," he said, pausing as he remembered their last encounter. "You know, I want to apologize for the last time I saw you, at the concert and all. I had no idea you were going to be there. I was hurt, and when the opportunity came up, I took it. It was weak of me."

Cami offered him a half-smile. "I deserved it, but you should know it was orchestrated by Mateo's uncle Aldo. He wanted me out of the picture, and for some reason, he thought that was the best way to do it. Anyway, it's over now. And look at you, so successful; I always knew you would make it."

Beau stood silent, reflecting on the woman who had unexpectedly entered his life years ago and left just as abruptly. Their silence was interrupted by Salty running up the moving sidewalk.

"Yo man, what the hell? I was in a fucking mob back there," Salty exclaimed, surprised to see Camille. "Yo, what are you doing here?" he asked, confused.

Cami began to answer when Beau interrupted, "She's moving back from Miami. This is her first day back. Welcome her home, man, damn." Salty looked at Beau, puzzled, but complied, "Welcome home, Cam. Glad to have you back," he said, still perplexed.

Cami nodded, "Thanks, Salt. I appreciate that."

The three of them stood in awkward silence until Salty decided to make his exit. "Hey man, I'm going to the car. These bitches are crazy around here."

Cami and Beau laughed as they watched Salty quickly walk away. Turning to Beau, Cami said, "Well, it was nice seeing you again. I need to find the kids. One of them is waiting on me, not sure which one got elected to pick Mama up."

Beau laughed at her comment. "It was really good seeing you. You should come to one of our local shows. Shoot me a message, and I'll get you a good seat," he offered.

Cami smiled, "I just may do that." They hugged, and Cami felt a moment of hesitation in her embrace. Letting go, she watched him walk away, stunned by the coincidence of their airport encounter.

Shaking her head, she gathered her things, murmuring to herself, "What are the odds?"

Chapter 9

2 Weeks Later

Cami nestled under the awning of her quaint A-frame home, her gaze fixed on the gentle splash of water in the man-made koi pond nestled in the quiet suburbs of Atlanta. The morning air was crisp, carrying with it the promise of a new day as she savored her coffee, the aroma blending with the quiet of her surroundings.

Just then, Annaliese's voice pierced the serene moment. Peeking her head out the door, she offered, "Do you want something to eat? I made bagels and cream cheese."

Cami turned, her response quick, a soft decline, "No thanks, I'm not really hungry."

But Annaliese, ever the caring mother, stepped outside, her hand finding a gentle rest on Cami's head. "Honey, you have to eat."

Cami took another sip of her coffee and shot her mom a look. "Please stop, I'm not hungry," she implored. She stared intently.

"I know. I'm just worried about you. Are you depressed? You know you have so much to be thankful for and look forward to," Annaliese expressed with concern.

"Mom, I'm fine. I'm just trying to adjust. I moved from Sunny Miami, the sounds of the city and ocean, to suburbia. It feels so remote. I just need to get used to the atmosphere here. I am trying to find some solace in this quiet place," Cami explained.

Annaliese gave Cami a half smile, knowing that she couldn't convince her to open up until she wanted to. "Okay, well, I'm going to go home. I've cleaned and organized some things in here. You know, honey, maybe if you start unpacking some of these boxes, it will get your mind off things," Annaliese suggested before leaving.

Cami sipped her coffee, staring at how the light rain made the water ripple over the pond. She found meaning in moments like these, pondering if life would be less stressful in a small pond rather than a vast ocean. Perhaps this is what she needed to be home, in Georgia, on a small piece of land surrounded by a few close people.

Snapping out of her reverie, she responded, "Mama, I will get to it. Go take care of Frank. I'll call you later. I think I am going to go see Daddy. I haven't seen him in a while and need to check on him."

Annaliese smiled at her daughter's words. Cami had always been a daddy's girl, yet her busy lifestyle and her dad's unsociable nature made their relationship seem incompatible at times. Nonetheless, they were alike in so many ways—both had tough exteriors and gypsy souls, craving freedom and adventures in their unique ways.

Cami's father was a quiet man who preferred the solitude of the country, living with his cats, far from the hustle of city life and the materialistic world. Cami often wondered how he found happiness in such a reclusive lifestyle, but she was beginning to see its appeal. Picking up the phone, she was greeted by his deep, familiar voice. "Hello," her dad answered sternly.

"Hey, Daddy, how are you?" she asked.

"I'm fine. Where the hell have you been? You haven't called since you moved back. I figured you'd be out here to see me by now," he replied in a tone mix of annoyance and concern.

Cami exhaled, feeling a mix of guilt and anticipation. "Well, that's why I'm calling. I was going to see if I could come out today. I'm just getting settled in and have some free time before I start working again next week," she explained, her voice eager.

Her father remained silent for a moment, likely processing her words. Then, sensing her need for connection, his tone softened. "Come on. I'll fix you a sandwich," he offered warmly.

Cami smiled, feeling a wave of relief and affection. She ended the call, grabbed her purse, and headed out the door, looking forward to the comfort of her father's presence and the simple pleasure of a shared meal.

****

Beau and Salty were settled in the studio, deeply engaged in their latest musical project, when Salty's memory jogged back to a recent, unexpected encounter. "Hey man, I've been meaning to ask you, how fucking weird was it bumping into Cami at the airport?" Salty inquired, his curiosity apparent.

Beau let out a laugh, shaking his head in disbelief. "Pretty fucking weird," he confirmed. "She actually tripped at the end of that moving sidewalk, face down. I immediately thought her ass looked familiar but couldn't see her face. I was like, there's no fucking way this could be her, and sure enough, she lifted her head."

Salty couldn't help but snicker at the recount, amazed by the coincidence. "Damn, man, the Universe is crazy," he remarked.

Beau, momentarily distracted from the mixing board, agreed, "It sure is," before returning his focus to their work.

Salty, still hanging on the story, waited for more. "So, what did she say?" he prodded.

Beau stopped what he was doing and sat back in his chair with a sly grin and said, "Nothing shocking; she and her Latin lover are no more. She has moved back to Atlanta. I don't know, man, and honestly, I don't care," he stated, his interest seemingly detached from the unexpected update on Cami's life.

Salty furrowed his brow, looking questioningly at Beau. "So you aren't going to try that again?" he asked. Beau's response was immediate and lighthearted, filled with laughter. "Hell no," he exclaimed, the amusement clear in his voice. But then, softening a bit, he added, "But I did tell her to come to one of our shows if she wanted to, and I did apologize for the incident in Miami."

That got a laugh out of Salty, who seemed to have expected as much. "Ummm huh, that's what I thought," he said, a knowing tone in his voice.

As the conversation shifted, Beau lit his joint and rolled over in his chair to grab a lighter. "No, bro, that ship has sailed," he asserted, passing the joint to Salty.

Salty, however, wasn't ready to let it go, his laughter punctuating his tease. "Yeah, sailed right back into the port," he joked.

Beau shot back with a quick-witted reply, "Yeah, I might gas her up a few times and send her back out to sea." The exchange was filled with laughter, showcasing their shared sense of corny humor.

As they returned their focus to the music, Beau found his thoughts wandering back to Cami and the complexity of their past. Despite his assurances and the humor shared with Salty, he knew convincing his friend was one thing; convincing himself, however, was another thing entirely.

****

Cami bit into the sandwich that her dad placed in front of her. "Wow, this is good. I haven't really had an appetite lately," Cami said, covering her mouth as she chewed and talked.

Peter looked at his daughter with his piercing green eyes. "What's been going on with you? You pack your things, move to Miami, and I get a few Facetime phone calls here and there. You know, I haven't actually seen your real face in a long time," her father stated with his deep voice.

Cami lowered her gaze, the piece of sandwich in her mouth suddenly feeling like a lump that was hard to swallow. She took a sip of water, gathering her thoughts before attempting to bridge the distance her absence had created.

"Daddy, I've just been caught up with Mateo. I know you hate to travel, and I should have come back to visit, but we had this business, and then I found out he was doing things he shouldn't have; there were some implications," Cami's voice started to crack. She did not want to explain the situation in Miami to her father.

Peter stared at his daughter inquisitively, his brow furrowed. "Implications? What kind of implications?" He asked firmly. He was not going to let it slide.

Cami took a deep breath, steeling herself for her father's reaction, which she anticipated would not be good. "Daddy, Mateo opened a business for me, you know, a cleaning business like we had in Atlanta. Except, this one employed beautiful women, and... I had no idea he was using it as a front for... essentially, a call girl operation. I truly had no clue," she confessed, the weight of her words hanging heavily in the air.

"Thank God Mateo had connections with politicians who couldn't afford to have their names dragged through the mud. He took all the blame. Somehow, I managed to come out of it without a scratch, legally speaking. But, Daddy, I couldn't stay in Miami after that. My business, my name, it was all tainted," Cami continued, her voice tinged with relief.

Peter, processing this bombshell, sat back, his gaze locked on his daughter. "Prostitution?!" This sounds like something out of a Hollywood movie. Are you serious? How could you possibly not have known about this?" he demanded, his voice rising with disbelief and concern.

"Daddy, I swear I had no idea. I thought we were living the American Dream. We got married, started a business, went on our honeymoon, and then... I found out Mateo had a love child. I left him, took over the business, and then all this chaos erupted. It's just been a mess," Cami broke down, tears streaming down her face as he started to fully realize the events of her recent life.

Despite his anger and disappointment, Peter's heart softened as he saw his daughter defeated and vulnerable. "I warned you about men from other countries. You just can't trust them," he lamented, his protective instincts kicking in.

Cami, despite the gravity of her situation, couldn't help but let out a chuckle at her dad's comment. "Daddy, you're Italian. Your father was from Italy, as were our mothers and our grandfathers before us; they were all good men," she reminded him gently, trying to lighten the mood.

Peter got up and poured his daughter a glass of homemade wine, clarifying his stance, "I am Italian, but I am not foreign. People like Mateo grow up differently; they learn how to charm trusting women like you, but they are also very dangerous. You have never taken my advice before. Take it now. Get back to your roots, where you belong. Find someone you can relate to and settle down. You have lived this jet-set life too long, and I promise that kind of life doesn't end well."

Cami shook her head, agreeing with her father. She knew her father's wise words held more truth than she cared to admit.

Chapter 10

One Week Later

Cami tussled with her keys and her phone, trying to get in the door, when her messenger lit up. Opening the message, she found it was Beau: "We are playing at the Atlanta Arts Center tonight. If you want to come, let me know. I'll get you and a friend in VIP." Hesitant, Cami pondered her response before deciding to call Heidi, an old friend from Atlanta.

"Hello?" Heidi answered.

"Hey girl, this is Cami. How are you?"

"Oh my God, Cami. I heard you were back in town! I've missed you so much. I knew you would move back eventually," Heidi exclaimed, her voice a mix of surprise and joy.

Cami felt a knot in her stomach, memories of the past years threatening to resurface. "Yeah, it's a long story, Heidi. I don't want to talk about it right now. But I was wondering if you want to go to a concert with me? You remember Beau from The MIXXX?"

Heidi's laughter came through the phone. "Yes, I remember. Wow, are you seeing him again? I can't believe he would even speak to you after the way you left him. Hell, I'm surprised I'm talking to you after you left me," she said, her tone teasing yet tinged with old hurt.

"No, Heidi, it's nothing like that. We've made our amends. He just asked if I wanted to come to one of his shows. I didn't want to go by myself and thought it would be fun to catch up. He said he would get us VIP. Maybe it's a chance to make up for lost time," Cami explained, hoping to mend bridges and create new memories with her old friend.

"Hell yeah, I do, I fucking love them. Let me arrange a sitter. I forgive you, by the way. When is it?" Heidi's excitement was palpable through the phone.

"It is tonight, at the Arts Center, at 7. I know that it is short notice, but I would love for you to come with me," Cami replied, her own excitement growing.

"I'm totally down; pick me up at around 6, and we will pre-game. You think your friend Kali will want to go?" Heidi asked, eager to make plans.

"Yeah, she is always up for a party, and now that I am on her turf, she will arrange a driver for us," Cami said, feeling a rush of anticipation.

Hanging up, Cami couldn't help but smile genuinely for the first time in ages. The music was already pulsating in her heart as she imagined the night ahead.

7 PM

Dropped off at the front of the huge building, the three women walked to the window. "Yes, my name is Camille Leone; I should be on the VIP list," Cami announced confidently.

The attendant slowly ran her finger down the list. "Yes, I see your name right here. You're on the guest list for Mr. Machado," she confirmed.

"That's me, and there should be two more spots for my friends here," Cami said, gesturing to Heidi and Kali. They were then shown to the VIP section overlooking the stage, a perfect vantage point for the evening.

"Damn, girl, you really hooked us up. Tequila, fruit, peanuts, you can't beat that shit," Heidi remarked, impressed by the setup.

Camille's thoughts drifted back to her first date with Beau. She vividly recalled the wine in plastic cups and the peanuts served to her at a small table backstage. Now, as she looked around the large venue, she was impressed by Beau's success. "He has really come a long way," she stated quietly, marveling at how far he had come.

Kali, ever the instigator of a good time, poured shots of tequila. "Fuck yeah, let's toast."

Cami didn't hesitate, raising her glass high and beginning their traditional toasting ritual. "Pain makes you braver, tears make you stronger, heartbreak makes you wiser, and tequila makes you forget that shit," she declared.

The ladies erupted in laughter; their carefree voices filled the air, a perfect prelude to the night's adventures. "Enough said," Heidi agreed just as the lights started to dim. Beau and Salty appeared on the stage, and the crowd's energy only grew, electrifying the atmosphere.

The duo kicked off with their new tracks, and immediately, the girls were on their feet, dancing and singing along, screaming the lyrics at the top of their lungs. Amidst the euphoria, Cami's mind briefly wandered to the last time she saw Beau on stage. It had been a humiliating experience, but she quickly shook off the painful memory, determined to forget the past.

As "The Mixxx" came to an end, Beau's voice cut through the noise. "We have one more new song out," he announced into the microphone. "It's a little bit different than anything we have done before. I hope you all like it; it is called 'Broken.'"

Salty's voice then took over, singing the words of a broken man, his heartaches, and the pain of trying to rebuild. The song struck a chord with Cami, and as her heart resonated with the lyrics, tears began to flow.

Noticing her distress, Heidi and Kali were quick to offer their support, wrapping their arms around her. "No, I don't want to do this right now. I just want to have fun," Cami protested through her tears. "It's ok, Cami. Just let it go. It's fine," Heidi reassured her. "I just can't believe all of this has happened. I feel so stupid," Cami confessed.

As the song came to an end and the lights began to brighten, Cami quickly wiped her tears away. She was about to grab her purse when she looked up to see Beau standing in the doorway. Heidi and Kali, sensing the need for privacy, started to make their way outside the VIP, leaving Cami and Beau to reconnect.

"We are going to head to the bar. Cami, do you want us to wait for you?" Heidi asked, turning around before leaving Cami behind.

"No, go ahead. I'll catch an Uber," Cami replied. As Kali and Heidi headed out, Kali whispered to Heidi, "We won't see that bitch for the rest of the night."

Beau settled into the plush couch in the VIP section and patted the cushion next to him, inviting Cami to sit down. With a half-smile, Cami approached and took her place beside him. Beau's concern was evident as he quickly noticed her state. "Have you been crying?" he inquired, looking at her with a mix of curiosity and concern.

Cami let out a half-hearted laugh, her emotions still raw. "Well, your new song kind of hit home. It spelled out the past two years of my life... and here I am, as broken as ever," she confessed, her vulnerability on full display.

Beau's response was filled with affection and understanding. "You're only broken if you choose to be. Do you want to talk about it?" he gently asked, showing his willingness to listen and support.

Cami shook her head slowly, a mix of sadness and resignation in her gesture. "No, I don't. You already know the details. You predicted it the day we broke up," she reminded him, referring to a painful shared memory.

Remembering the day all too well, Beau felt a tinge of guilt. "I am sorry. I wasn't exactly in a good place that day, and I was hurt, but everything happens for a reason," he reflected, attempting to offer some solace amidst the painful memories.

Curious, Cami found herself asking about Beau's current romantic life despite her reservations. "Are you seeing anyone?" she blurted out. She wanted to sound casual, but her curiosity was evident in her tone.

Beau, taken aback but with a humorous twist, replied, "Well, yes, I see my manager, my friends, my dog, my kids... I see a lot of people. You, I see you." His playful response lightened the mood, drawing a laugh from Cami.

"You know what I mean, Beau," she nudged him, a smile breaking through her gloomy mood. Beau's smile, showcasing his beautiful straight teeth and sexy demeanor, momentarily took Cami back to the days of their past romance, igniting a mix of emotions within her.

"No, Cami, I'm not seeing anyone exclusively. You women are hard to deal with," Beau admitted with a playful tone.

Cami responded with a hopeful smile and a light laugh. "Yeah, I guess we are, but you men are no walk-in-the-park either," she retorted, matching his light-heartedness.

Beau then placed his hand on Cami's knee, signaling a comforting familiarity between them. "It's really nice to have you back. Do you want to go to dinner sometime, just as friends?" he suggested gently.

Cami looked at Beau, a bit resigned to his emphasis on "friends," yet she agreed, her voice tinged with hope. "Yes, I would like that. Friends and dinner sounds good to me," she said, optimistic about the proposition.

In a moment of tenderness, Beau lightly touched Cami's face and gave her a light kiss. "Would you like a ride to the bar? I can take you to Kali and Heidi," he offered. Cami glanced at her watch, her mind drifting to the thought of her cozy bed. "No, I'm going to go home. But I've had a great time. Thank you for inviting me," she appreciated Beau's gesture warmly.

Beau stood and offered his hand, a gesture of chivalry. "Come on, I'll take you home," he said, prompting Cami to take his hand, albeit with a hint of reluctance. "It's just a ride, Cam, no funny business," he reassured her, sensing her hesitation. Together, they headed to the SUV, enveloped in a silence that was comfortable and familiar. The scent of his cologne, the chosen music, and the cool night air brought back memories, making Cami feel as if she was reliving a moment from the past.

As the SUV came to a stop, Cami looked at Beau with affection and gratitude. "Thank you, Beau," she said sincerely. "You're welcome, beautiful. I'll call you, that is, if you want me to," Beau responded with a hopeful smile.

Cami nodded, her heart agreeing before her words could follow. "Yes, I would love that," she said, her voice carrying a mixture of relief and anticipation.

Closing the SUV door behind her, Cami felt a sense of closure wash over her, soothing the remnants of past heartaches with Beau. She watched him drive away, a chapter ending, yet another perhaps just beginning.

Chapter 11

Cami poured her morning cup of coffee, her thoughts drifting to Beau and their recent conversation. As she reached for her phone, a new message popped up: "Good Morning Beautiful."

A smile spread across her face—it was from Beau. She quickly replied, "Good morning to you, handsome." The exchange sparked a wave of nostalgia. As she eagerly awaited his response, the familiar text bubbles appeared.

"I was serious about our friendly dinner date. Are you interested?" Reading this, Cami's smile widened at the thought of spending time alone with Beau, catching up on the past few years.

"Absolutely, when and where?" she texted back.

"Meet me at the bar at Ray's around 6:30," came his reply. Cami paused, surprised by the venue choice and somewhat taken aback that Beau hadn't offered to pick her up.

Reminding herself that this was just a friendly date, she responded, "OK, see you then."

Meanwhile, Beau stepped outside to enjoy the morning sun. He closed his eyes, letting the warmth of the rays wash over him, and lit a rolled blunt, inhaling deeply. "Yo man, you're up early," Salty called out from the doorway of the home he now shared with Beau.

The demands of touring and making music had led them to share space, with Salty having a spacious studio built beside Beau's sprawling ranch-style home where he spent most of his time working on music.

"Yeah, man, it's nice outside. You want to hit this?" Beau passed the blunt to Salty with a contented grin.

"What's that shit-eating grin for?" Salty inquired, taking the blunt with a curious look.

Beau chuckled lightly. "I don't know, man, I'm just happy."

Salty took a long drag, holding the smoke in, then teased, "That's an 'I'm about to get some ass' grin."

Beau laughed off the comment. "Naw, man, just happy." His mind wandered back to the conversation with Cami. A flicker of doubt crept in, prompting him to seek advice from his longtime friend. "Hey Salt, remember when I said I wouldn't revisit a relationship with Cami?"

Salty nodded, not surprised by the confession. "Yeah, man, I knew that was a lie," he said knowingly.

Beau furrowed his brow. "I don't mean like a romantic relationship; I mean like a friendly one. I'm taking her to dinner, just as friends. I'm not even picking her up; she's just meeting me at a bar," he explained with conviction.

"You can sell yourself that lie if you want to, Beau, but don't go getting yourself caught up in that mess again—we have work to do. As nice and fine as she is, she's dangerous, man. That will be a treacherous road to travel. She's like a butterfly: unpredictable, never knowing where she's going to land. Although, I will say we got a hit song out of it," Salty added with a wry smile.

Beau smirked, shaking his head in reluctant agreement. "That we did, my friend," he conceded, a hint of disappointment in his voice at the truth his friend had laid bare.

Later, Cami walked into Ray's bar, immediately taken by the ambient lighting and the soft classical music that filled the air, enhancing the bar's romantic vibe. She strutted to the bar, hung her purse on a hook underneath, and greeted the handsome bartender with a bright smile.

"Good evening, I'll have a glass of pinot grigio," she requested. As the bartender nodded and went to fetch her drink, Cami's eyes scanned the room. They brightened when she spotted Beau entering. Dressed in black pants and a polo shirt that hugged his physique, his tattoos vividly wrapping his arms like sleeves, he approached with a confident stride and a warm smile.

"Well, hello, Ms. Cami, how are you?" he greeted, planting a light kiss on her cheek before sitting down beside her and signaling the bartender, "I'll have a bourbon and coke."

As they sipped their drinks, Cami and Beau reminisced about their past, deliberately avoiding any mention of Mateo. The night was filled with shared laughter and playful touches. Eventually, Beau glanced at his watch, noticing both the late hour and the emptying room. "Wow, it's late," he remarked, a brief silence falling between them.

"You know, time flies when you're having fun," Cami responded, laughing off her cliché with a hint of embarrassment.

Beau hesitated, then made a daring suggestion. "Why don't we go back to my place? The kids aren't there, and I'm sure Salty will be in the studio."

Cami lowered her gaze, contemplating the proposition. The wine had warmed her blood, and the evening's reconnection with Beau had stirred something within her. "Sure, why not? It's not like it's another notch in my belt," she quipped, her voice playful.

The two exchanged a knowing, playful glance, chuckling softly. Beau suggested, "Follow me home?"

Cami arrived right behind Beau, parking her car and waiting for his cue to come inside. He walked to her car door, peering in through the window before he lifted the latch and opened the door. "So, you coming in?" he asked, his voice light but inviting.

Feeling a bit awkward, Cami stepped out of the car and followed Beau to the front door. As he fumbled for his keys, a sense of nostalgia swept over her, reminding her of their first night together in Atlanta. She chuckled, a sound that felt warm and familiar.

"What are you laughing at?" Beau turned to her with a curious look.

"You, always fumbling for your keys," she teased, her smile brightening the night.

Beau laughed in response, the tension easing between them as they stepped inside. Cami looked around at the humble, welcoming interior of his home. Suddenly, Beau turned to her, his hands gently cupping her face as he leaned in for a kiss. The touch of his soft lips reignited old passions, stirring memories of their shared history.

Caught in the moment, they found themselves in a whirlwind of renewed affection, their clothing falling away as they moved together toward the bedroom. Their embrace was passionate and urgent, their connection deepening as they fell onto the bed.

Beau's kisses traced a path from her head to her toes, each touch reigniting forgotten desires. Beau kissed her body until he looked her in the eye, remembering the girl from years earlier; he never left her gaze before entering her body. Their lovemaking was slow and passionate, leading them into the morning.

****

Cami woke to the sunlight streaming through the windows, its brightness causing her to squint as she sat up. She was alone in the unfamiliar room, clearly Beau's, but he was nowhere in sight. The sound of a flushing toilet broke the silence, and soon Beau reentered the bedroom.

"Good morning. Did you sleep well?" he asked. His tone was light, but his smile was only half-formed as he slid into his black jogging pants.

"Yes, if you call that sleeping, I guess so," Cami replied, sensing a certain coldness in his demeanor that she couldn't quite place. "Do you have a busy day?"

Beau turned his back to her as he scrolled through his phone. "Yes, Cami, I actually do. I need to be at the studio in an hour," he stated matter-of-factly.

Feeling the disconnect, Cami took this as her cue to leave. She began gathering her clothes, which were neatly folded on the bedside table, pointed out by Beau. With a lump forming in her throat from the abruptness of his tone, she tried small talk.

"Do you think I could see Salty before I go? I love catching up with him; he always knows how to make me laugh."

"No, Cami, we won't be seeing Salty today," Beau replied with a half-grin before quickly exiting the room.

Confused by his sudden detachment, Cami followed him, trailing a few steps behind. "Is something wrong, Beau?" she asked as he stood at the counter, breaking up marijuana and placing it in a grinder without making eye contact.

"Nothing is wrong, Camille. I just have a busy day," he replied curtly, focusing on his task.

Cami decided not to press further, sensing the futility. On her way to the door, she stopped with a confused look back at Beau. "Call me when you're not busy," she said, a mix of hope and resignation in her voice.

Beau came around the corner to the door as Cami stepped out onto the porch. He kissed her on the forehead. "I'll call you Ms. Cami," he said softly, using the endearing nickname he had given her during their dating years. While this brought a fleeting sense of relief, deep down, Cami felt a nagging doubt that she might not hear from Beau Machado again.

Chapter 12

One Week Later

Cami sat by her koi pond, watching the fish swim in circles. A familiar feeling of being trapped in a never-ending cycle of redundant day-to-day life swept over her. She had waited patiently for a week for Beau to call her, not daring to reach out to him.

"Why would he ghost me?" she thought to herself. The more she pondered it, the more determined she became to understand his actions.

Speaking aloud, she declared, "You know what, I didn't ask for this. I didn't even want to talk to you at the airport that day. And why ask me to come to one of your concerts, apologize, just to fuck me, and never speak to me again? That is so messed up. It's not like I want a relationship; I'm not some stage-five clinger."

Cami grabbed her phone and pulled up Beau's number. She started typing a text, deleting it five different times before finally hitting the call button. It went straight to voicemail. Her blood began to boil, not over the rejection but the fact that he drew her in only to spit her out.

"I would have been just fine being your friend but fuck it. Now, what do I have to lose?" she muttered to herself, grabbing her purse and heading to Beau's studio in the city.

On her way to the studio, Cami called her friend Heidi. "Hey girl, what are you doing?" she asked as soon as Heidi answered.

Before Heidi could respond, Cami erupted into a tirade. "You know what this motherfucker Beau has done? He ghosted me! Can you believe this shit? Like, I am one of his backstage groupies. I don't get it, but I'm going to get it in about 15 minutes," Cami blurted out.

Heidi, taken aback by Cami's anger, had to ask, "Whoa, Cam, what the fuck are you about to do? Do we need a shovel? This sounds serious; you sound like we're about to bury a body."

Cami chuckled, her laughter laced with determination. "I am so fucking mad right now; I truly hate men, Heidi. If I could get away with it, I swear I would murder all of them, starting with Mateo. I am tired of being the docile bitch. Who cares if he thinks I'm crazy? I'm going down to his studio, and I'm going to ask him, 'What the fuck did I do to deserve this?'" Cami said fervently.

Heidi laughed and said, "Well, other than cheat on him, leave him, move away, marry someone else, nothing really."

Cami remained silent at Heidi's truthful comment and started to calm herself, although she had no response until Heidi asked, "Cami, are you there? I didn't mean to upset you, girl, but men are vengeful. Maybe he just got you back, and maybe you should take it."

Cami finally drew her breath, accepting the truth in Heidi's words, and responded, "Yeah, you know what? You're probably right, Heidi, but fuck, I feel like that humiliating birthday party in Miami was payback enough. I thought he and I were in a different place. I'm going down there, but I am going to calm down first and just ask him what happened."

Heidi could hear the confusion in her friend's voice and felt compassion for her, knowing she was going to embarrass herself but also knowing there was no talking her out of it. "Ok, Cam, go down and get your answers if you think that will make you feel better, but when you leave feeling embarrassed and shocked by what you hear, I'll be here, tequila shots and all."

"I hear you; I'll let you know how it goes," Cami said, disconnecting the call. She pulled into the parking lot, her heart pounding.

Cami slowly walked to the studio situated in a small alley in downtown Atlanta. As she tried to find the entrance, a group of young men wearing all black approached her.

"What's a fine little mama like yourself doing down here?" One of the men looked Cami up and down. She could feel her heart pounding as her survival instincts kicked in.

"I'm looking for someone, a rapper. His name is Beau. This is his studio. He knows I'm coming. I'm sure he will be out in a minute," Cami said, her voice rattling with fear.

One of the three men slowly approached her, backing her against a wall. The man ran his fingers across Cami's hairline; she quickly turned her head as he moved his lips closer to hers. "Macho's studio moved, little mama. He's not coming to look for you. If you were his girl, you would know that, but if you like, you can be my girl. They call me Redbone."

Cami tried desperately to slowly reach into her purse for her mace when she heard a man's voice, "Hey man, what the fuck are you doing?"

Cami saw a man approach, dressed in casual business attire. Redbone backed off and laughed. "Oh, what's up, Cash? We were just helping this young lady find her way to the studio. Says she is looking for Macho. We just had to inform her that Macho's studio moved. She won't be finding no Beau Machado here."

Cash looked at Redbone and his posse, then back at Cami. He could see the fear etched on her face. "She is with me. I'll take her to Macho. Now get the fuck out of here," Cash muttered intently.

Redbone flashed his gun as a show of force, feeling disrespected by Cash's demand. Without hesitation, Cash quickly pulled his gun from the back of his pants and stuck it to Redbone's face. "I said get the fuck out of here, Red."

Redbone quickly raised his hands. "Okay, okay, but I'll remember this, Cash."

Cash lowered the gun, maintaining eye contact. "Good, you should, motherfucker." The men slowly backed away and retreated.

Cash turned to Cami. "You okay? What are you doing down here? This is no place for a woman like you. Did he say you were looking for Macho?"

Cami started to fumble for her keys, clearly rattled by the experience. "Yes, but I am going to leave. You are right; I have no business down here," she stated fearfully.

Cash immediately felt pity for her, seeing her terror. "Macho has moved studios. We built one in a nicer location on a nicer side of town for this very reason. I was just here picking up a few things. And by the way, you are lucky I was here. There is no telling what they would have done to you," Cash said intently.

Cami hung her head, thinking of Heidi's words, when Cash decided to introduce himself. "I am Cash Davidson, by the way. And who are you?" he asked, extending his hand.

Cami slowly lifted her delicate, shaking hand. "I am Camille Leone. I am a friend of Beau's. He didn't know I was coming down here. I just wanted to speak with him about something," she stated.

Cash pulled out his cell phone and put it to his ear. "Yo, Macho, what's up, man?" Cami was mortified, shaking her head, trying to get Cash to disconnect the call, but it was too late. He hit the speaker button so Cami could hear the conversation.

"Yo man, what's up with you? Where you are, you're late," Beau said.

Cash hesitated. "Look, man, I found this girl down here in the alley looking for you. She about got her ass killed. Thank God I was here," Cash said.

Beau remained silent for a moment, then responded, "Black hair, fine, short, green eyes, probably wearing heels, southern accent?"

Cash smiled at Cami as she rolled her eyes. "Yeah, man, that's her," Cash chuckled.

"Okay, man, bring her here. I appreciate you looking out for her," Beau said kindly.

"No problem. See you soon," Cash disconnected the call and looked at Cami. "So, do you want to follow me?"

Cami lowered her head and stared at the ground, finally mustering the courage to speak through her shame. "Maybe, I don't know; I shouldn't have caused you trouble," she said.

Cash smirked. "Well, maybe you should since you have caused me this much trouble."

Cami laughed through her apology. "I am so sorry. Sometimes I don't think, and I just thought that... Anyway, I don't know what I was thinking," she said.

Cash hit the unlock button on his blacked-out F150. Cami heard the chirp of the unlock. "Follow me," he said.

Cami shamefully walked to her BMW and plopped down in the seat, still in shock from the events of the past 30 minutes. She started her car and followed Cash out of the parking lot.

Cami pulled in slowly behind Cash and parked her car. She could see Beau waiting outside the newly built studio on the outskirts of Atlanta. Hesitating before exiting the car, she found herself at a loss for words; everything she wanted to say to Beau had vanished from her mind.

Cash and Cami walked toward Beau. "Here she is, man. Little Red Riding Hood saved her from the wolves," Cash said with a chuckle. Beau and Cami laughed, but then an awkward silence settled over them. Cash broke the silence, "I'll let you two talk. It was nice meeting you, Ms. Camille."

Cami and Cash's eyes locked awkwardly, and she realized she hadn't responded. "Thank you, Mr. Davidson. Really, I appreciate it, and again, I apologize for the trouble," she stuttered.

Beau noticed the exchange between the two and started to feel a bit territorial, motioning for Cash to go. He then turned to Cami, staring at her without a word.

"What?" Cami asked, frowning.

Beau put his hands on his hips and smirked. "What were you thinking, Cami? You can't just pull up in the middle of downtown Atlanta. You're not a gangster, and you surely can't be as naïve as you're acting right now. I thought you were smarter than that."

Cami felt offended by his comment. "Beau, I am not naive. You ghosted me, and I wanted to talk. I don't understand this. I am not asking to be in a relationship, but I did think you were my friend," she said, her voice cracking.

Beau rubbed his face, the stress of the conversation wearing on him. He blurted out, "Cami, I am married, but we are separated. I married her shortly after you left. I have another child, but she lives in Texas. It's very complicated, and I just can't get involved with you like that. What we had was special, but to be quite honest, you ruined that for us. I thought cutting you off completely was the best way, but I see now it wasn't. I do owe you an explanation, so this is it."

Cami stood there speechless, her entire speech a blank page in her mind. Without a word, she turned around and headed for her car.

Beau chased after her. "Cami, please wait! I'm really sorry!" he yelled.

Cami continued to walk to her car, quickly opening the door and driving away.

Beau watched Cami drive away with a sense of regret but knew he had made the right decision. Cash, who had been watching the exchange from the doorway of the studio, noticed the stress etched on Beau's face. As Beau approached, Cash inquired, "Hey man, who is she to you?"

Beau hurried past Cash, mumbling swiftly, "No one."

Cash watched Camille drive away, intrigued by her beauty and their instant connection. "No one, huh?" he softly said to himself. Cash pulled out his phone, went straight to Instagram, typed in her name, *Camille Leone,* found her immediately, and requested to follow.

****

Cami swung her BMW into Heidi's driveway and burst through the door. "Heidi, Heidi, where are you?" she called out frantically. Heidi emerged from the back of her house. "What? What the fuck happened?"

Cami went straight to Heidi's kitchen and poured a shot of tequila, shooting it back as she braced herself on the counter with both hands. Heidi's eyes were wide with curiosity. "Spit it out, Camille. Tell me what the fuck is going on?" she exclaimed.

Cami hung her head and let out a scream. "Fuck, Heidi! I was almost assaulted downtown. Thank God there was this man, fine as hell, by the way, who came out looking like an Iron Man superhero to save me. Thank God! But that's not the best part. Beau is married—separated, but married nonetheless—and he has another child." With that, Cami threw back another shot of tequila.

Heidi stood there, stunned. "Shut the fuck up, bitch. Are you serious?" she asked, shocked by the revelation. She threw back a shot of tequila, following suit with Cami.

"Oh, I have never been more fucking serious in my life. She lives in Texas, thank God. Fuck me, I just don't understand men. I'm fucking done. When I say I am done, that means I am fucking done. Fuck this shit. I am out on men—no more men for me," Cami exclaimed, lighting a cigarette.

Heidi opened the door. "Please, not in the house. Let's go to the pool. I'll bring the drinks," she offered, waving through the smoke.

Cami walked to the nearest lounge chair and dragged on her cigarette, thankful for the drink Heidi offered. Heidi took her place next to Cami. "So, what about this Iron Man? Did I hear you say he was fine?"

Cami looked at Heidi, confused, feeling as though Heidi hadn't heard a word she said. "What?" she asked, staring at Heidi in disbelief, shocked by her disinterest in her near-death experience, and her only curiosity was the sexiness of her knight and shining armor, finding herself speechless once again.

The two women burst into laughter at the ridiculousness of the drama that had etched its way into Cami's life. Through tears of laughter, Cami screamed, "You can't make this shit up."

Chapter 13

Two Months Later

Cami found herself spending more time with her friends, reacclimating to "single" life, and dating a handful of men, but she couldn't feel the passion she had with Beau or Mateo. On a warm summer's day, Heidi, Kali, and Cami showed up on the beach in Puerto Rico, sipping Pina Coladas and enjoying the endless possibilities of summer.

Heidi, lounging and soaking in the sun, asked, "Hey, Cami, what about that Cash Davidson guy you met a couple of months ago at Beau's studio?"

Kali, curious and intrigued by the name, chimed in, "Oh, Cash, is that his name? Do tell, ladies. Sounds interesting," she said, tossing her hair back with her ears wide open.

Cami chuckled at her friends, laying back in her chair and letting the sun warm her face. She recalled her encounter and gave the latest update. "He requested that I follow him on Instagram. I accepted but never thought much more about it. I will have to say he was fine—salt-and-pepper hair, beautiful hazel eyes, dark skin. A classy, more mature look, I guess you could say," Cami recalled.

Kali, even more intrigued, began to probe. "When you say more mature, do you mean older or rich?" she asked.

"I mean both. He was older and appeared to have money—or at least a little bit older than me, maybe in his late 40s," Cami stated, trying to find the right words.

Kali sat up in her chair, stunned by the revelation. "You mean to tell me you met a fine, older, rich gentleman, and you spent the past few months wasting your time on peanut dick losers?" Kali belted out.

Cami, offended, retorted, "Look, Kali, after Beau and Mateo, I decided to take a different approach. I thought dating a more average man was a safer bet, okay? I'm trying to get away from looks, money, music, and drugs."

Kali and Heidi burst into laughter. "Bitch! The last thing you want is broke and average. Give me your phone right now," Kali screamed.

Heidi quickly grabbed Cami's phone. "Give me your code," Heidi demanded.

Cami reluctantly gave Heidi the code, who quickly went to Cash's Instagram page. "Wow, have you lost your fucking mind? This man is a music producer, entrepreneur, master of tracks, and separated. Let's not forget fine as hell, and he saved your life," Heidi exclaimed.

Kali quickly grabbed the phone. "Let me see that." She examined the pictures and pulled up the direct messages on Instagram, quickly typing a message to Cash unbeknownst to Cami. "Hi, Cash, this is Camille Leone. We met a few months ago at the recording studio. Remember, you saved my life. Anyway, I was hoping I could take you out for a drink—my way of saying thank you."

"There, it's done," Kali said as she tossed the phone onto Cami's chair.

Cami, confused and unaware, picked up her phone. "What do you mean, 'done'?" Kali and Heidi laughed.

"I just sent him a message from you," Kali announced.

Cami swiftly picked up her phone and read the message. "Oh my God, you bitches, I swear I am going to kill both of you," Cami screamed, picking up a handful of sand and playfully tossing it at her friends.

****

Cash moved his fingers across the soundboard as Beau and Salty belted out their latest track. Unable to find the perfect beat and tired from the long day, he suggested, "Hey guys, let's take a five-minute break." Salty and Beau gladly retreated from the microphone. Cash, intrigued by the dinging of his phone, opened his Instagram messages to see a new message from Camille Leone. With a sly grin, he read it under his breath.

As Beau walked back into the studio, Cash motioned for him to come into the sound room. "You remember a couple of months ago, when that girl, 'no one' as you called her, Camille Leone, came to the old studio?" Cash asked with a knowing look.

Beau furrowed his brow. "Yeah, I do. How can I forget? That 'no one' is my ex-girlfriend, but it was over as quickly as it began. We hooked up briefly after she got back, but it didn't work out. Why do you ask?" Beau inquired.

Cash spun around in his chair and held the phone up to Beau's face. Beau squinted to read the message. Sitting back in his chair, trying to keep his emotions in check, Beau lit a cigarette.

"Looks like she wants to thank you for saving her life, I guess. Go for it, dude," he said casually.

Cash, pleased with Beau's blessing but not wanting to cause friction, asked, "Are you sure, man? Just drinks, nothing more. Would that be a problem?"

Beau took another drag of his cigarette and finished his water. "No, man, why not? She's free to do what she wants. I have no say in that. But what I do have a say in is what the fuck I am going to eat today. I am starving. I'll be back. You two want anything?" Beau asked.

Salty and Cash declined the offer, but Salty knew his friend all too well and could see the stress on his face. Beau walked out of the studio, quickly making his way to the parking lot. Unable to wait, he dialed Cami's number.

Meanwhile, Kali, Cami, and Heidi sauntered to an outside bar situated on the beach. The three women were laughing hysterically at the day's events and their drunken stupor when Cami received a call. "Holy shit, why the fuck would Beau be calling me?" Cami exclaimed as she looked down at her phone.

The women were suddenly struck with curiosity, watching Cami's phone ring and Beau's name flash across the screen. Heidi broke their silence. "Answer it," she stated curiously.

"No, I'm not answering it. What the fuck would he be calling me for?" Cami said when she remembered the text Kali had sent to Cash. "Oh my God, I bet Cash told him about the text," Cami exclaimed.

Kali started to chuckle, scoffing at the audacity of Beau possibly being upset with Cami. "So fucking what? Answer it. I'd like to hear what he has to say."

Cami rolled her eyes at the thought. She had not spoken to Beau since the day she walked away from his studio, but curiosity set in. Reluctantly, she answered, "Hello," she said softly. Heidi and Kali leaned in to listen.

"Yo, Cami, this is Beau," he said, urgency in his tone.

"Yeah, I know who it is. Can you hold on just a minute?" she said confidently, trying to shield the snickers of Heidi and Kali. Cami shooed the girls away. Kali and Heidi, disappointed that they could not be part of the drama, went to the bar to order a drink.

After Cami secured a private place to talk, she sipped her red wine and asked again, "Yeah, what's up? I am in Puerto Rico with the girls. We are out having cocktails and wine. You know how that goes, so how can I help you?" She asked in a professional tone.

Beau didn't waste any time with his questions. "What the fuck, Cami? I was in the studio with Cash, and he said he got a message from you. He's my producer. Can't you find a man somewhere else?" he retorted, anger laced in his voice.

Cami, offended and disgusted by the accusation, quickly replied, "Whoa, whoa, whoa, mister. First and foremost, yes, I can find a man anywhere. And for your fucking information, I did not send that message—Kali did. You know how impulsive she is. Before I knew it, she made it her mission to set me up. So, I'll accept your apology now. Don't worry, I'll wait for it," she said angrily.

Beau was at a loss for words. Silence lingered on his end. "Hello, are you there?" Cami asked.

"Yes, I am here. I just thought that you were hitting on my producer, and it pissed me off—not that it matters. I just didn't like it, I guess," Beau said, with a hint of sadness in his reaction.

Cami, flattered by his jealousy, remembered the heart-breaking conversation at the studio and quickly found her voice. "Yeah, you're right, Beau. It doesn't matter. And if he responds, I will respectfully ask you, may I have a drink with your friend Cash? I am single, and, honestly, I at least owe him a drink—he did practically save my life."

Beau stood in the parking lot with the phone glued to his ear, shocked by Cami's admission of interest in Cash. However, he knew he couldn't stop them. Hesitantly, he gave her his blessing. "You know what, Cami? Go out with him if you want to. I know that you have been through a lot. Maybe Cash would be a change of pace for you," he stated, his voice laced with compassion.

Cami was taken aback and a bit saddened by how quickly he gave up. "Well, thank you, Beau. That is awfully nice of a gangster such as yourself giving me permission to date," she stated with sarcasm. "And by the way, can you not mention Mateo and that whole situation to him? It's embarrassing and painful, and I never want to repeat it again," Cami added with disdain in her voice.

Beau laughed. "You really are a smartass. And no, I will not mention that to him. I would prefer not to give Mateo Vega one moment of my breath. Honestly, Cami, I hoped that we could remain friends," he said sincerely.

Cami's heart fluttered at his sincere words. She tried to swallow the lump that sat in her throat. "I would like that, Beau," she said, fighting back tears. At that moment, she knew that Beau's love for her was truly gone. She felt the transition in their relationship and the final chapter of their love affair closing.

Three Weeks Later

Cami sat wrapped in her soft blanket, feeling content being alone for the first time. She gave her new pet, a fluffy gray kitten, a pat on the head and watched the fire crackle in the fireplace. She was finally secure in her own skin—single, independent, and happy with her new job.

Her children all had lives of their own in Atlanta. Gabriella was a marketing rep, Michael was an internet sales manager for a sprawling car dealership, and Anthony, a straight-A, partying frat boy in college. Annaliese and Frank were settled in a high-rise condo, enjoying their retirement in downtown Buckhead and the tranquility of simplicity.

Cami's thoughts drifted back to Mateo, a time in her life that her mind often circled back to. She wondered what kind of father he was, if he still loved her, or if he even thought of her at all. Their sex life was unmatched, and the memory of it sometimes made Cami shudder. She mourned the loss of that connection with a man. Lost deep in her thoughts, she sipped her wine and smiled at the sweet kitten purring around her fingertips when her phone pinged.

Wondering who it could be, she picked up her phone to see a message from Cash Davidson. It had been over two weeks since Kali sent the infamous text, and she had assumed he was not interested. Intrigued, she opened the message. It read, "Hi Camille, I received your message a couple of weeks ago. I'll take you up on that drink if you're still interested."

Cami smiled excitedly and thought out her response. What took him so long? she wondered. Pouring herself another glass of wine, she flipped through the channels, glancing back and forth at her phone, contemplating whether or not to respond. She finally picked up the phone and texted back, "Sure, why not? When are you free?"

Cash quickly responded, "Friday sound good? And since it's 'just drinks,' do you want to meet me at that little jazz bar on the corner of Peachtree? The Scarlet Letter?"

Cami smirked at the name of the bar, not allowing her superstitious nature to ruin the moment. She swiftly responded, "Seven o'clock?"

The bubble response was immediate, "Sounds good. See you then."

Cami tossed her phone aside, gulped down the last drop of her wine, and headed to bed, a smile playing on her lips.

Chapter 14

Friday

7:00 PM

Cami pulled into the parking lot of the Scarlett Letter jazz bar. She stared at the brightly lit red sign and shook her head again at the coincidence—the woman who had been on the front lines to destroy her marriage to Mateo seemed to be sending her a message from afar. Cami snickered and began digging in her purse for lip gloss, meticulously gliding it across her lips. She smacked her lips and took one last glance in the mirror before heading inside.

The ambiance inside was warm and inviting, with dim lighting casting a cozy glow. The soulful sound of the saxophone calmed her nerves as she walked through the front entrance. Her eyes quickly found an alluring man with salt-and-pepper hair neatly cut around his ears. His white collared shirt, unbuttoned at the top, had a relaxed fit over his slim physique, and he wore light blue dress pants. He threw his hand up and waved her over to the bar.

Cami went to the bar and immediately started searching for a hook under the counter to hang her purse. Cash quickly noticed her short black-and-white polka dot dress and high heels. "You look like the Italian version of Pretty Woman," Cash said, pulling out her seat and offering his hand as she stepped up to the large barstool.

"Thank you, that's very sweet," she said, adjusting her dress and situating herself on the stool. Cash sat down beside her, still smiling.

"You are very welcome. Can I get you a drink?" he asked.

"Yes, a glass of Merlot would be nice," she said lightly, her nerves palpable.

Cash noticed a slight awkwardness. "It's okay, I don't bite, Ms. Leone," he said with a smile.

Cami gave Cash a side-eye and took a sip of her wine. With perfect form, she retorted, "Well, that's disappointing. I was kind of hoping you did," she said sarcastically.

Cash laughed out loud, somewhat shocked at her quick wittiness.

Cami jumped right in, "So, first and foremost, Mister Davidson, I want to thank you for saving me that afternoon at the studio. That was a very scary moment, and you rescued me. I was going to buy you a drink, but your offer expired, so I am happy you reached out," she said, her smile infectious.

Cash smirked, enjoying her raw humor. "So that means I am picking up the tab?" he asked knowingly.

Cami sipped her wine. "Yes, it does. Unless you're broke, I am sure they wouldn't mind if I washed dishes in the back."

They chuckled at the light-hearted joking when Cash took a more serious approach. "So, tell me about yourself. Beau didn't say much other than you two have dated and maybe had an encounter here and there."

Cami broke her eye contact and stared at her glass, thinking of the best and quickest way to describe herself and avoid any questions about her recent past.

"Well, I have three grown children, two and a half divorces—the third was annulled. I recently owned my own business, but it failed. I am a marketing agent here in Atlanta, and yes, Beau and I dated. It was a short-lived relationship, but we are friends, and that's about it. Nothing exciting, really," Cami said with confidence, hoping Cash would not probe further.

But he wanted more. "So, where did you grow up? Where did you go to school? Did you go to college? What is your favorite food? Color? And why in the world would someone want to divorce you?"

Cami was bemused by the barrage of questions. "Wow, that's a lot. So, let me sum it up. I grew up here in Atlanta. Yes, I went to college. Sushi is my favorite food, yellow is my favorite color, and who said anyone divorced me?" she questioned, giving him a sly look.

Cash took a swig of his beer. "Good point; all makes sense now," he said.

Cami could feel her anxiety rising and quickly asked, "So what about you? What's your story?"

Cash took another long swig of his beer, contemplating his response. "I don't know if I want to go into that right now. I really like you, but you may grab your shit and run," he laughed.

Cami smiled. "Try me," she said, ready to take it all in.

Cash started to unfold a tale of adultery, a bitter custody battle, family and friends pitted against each other, and two young children caught in the middle. Cami sat silent, listening, feeling the pain in every detail—a middle-aged man forced to start over, who desperately missed his children.

As Cash concluded his story, he looked at Cami, fully expecting her to excuse herself. "So if you want to walk away, go ahead now because I know it's a lot."

Cami felt so much empathy and compassion. She couldn't control herself; she leaned in and gave him a soft kiss, which he gladly reciprocated. Cash's blood started to warm, and when Cami sat back down and looked at him, he couldn't help but ask, "You want to get out of here? I have a studio apartment on a high rise not far from here. Nothing crazy, just private."

Cami knew what private meant but was happy to accept his offer. "Why not? It's not like I am trying to protect my reputation," she chuckled.

Cash laughed, starting to feel excited, and waved the bartender over. "Check, please."

Cami followed Cash to his high-rise building in Buckhead. On the ride up, an awkward silence fell between them. Cami broke the ice and said, "Don't get all silent on me now. You've got me here; now entertain me."

Cash gave her a sly grin and a funny laugh, his accent that of a quick-talking Cajun. "I'll entertain you alright."

Cami and Cash walked through the doors into a pristine, minimalistic scene. With the flick of a switch, a fireplace lit up. Cash walked over to a vintage record player and started to play Frank Sinatra. Cami responded, "Very romantic. Nice touch. I haven't heard that one since my grandmother passed; Sinatra was her favorite."

Cash grinned, "I love Frank Sinatra, along with an entire genre of music," he said, handing her a glass of Merlot.

Cami found herself wandering around the small studio, looking at the pictures of his children, parents, and a wall of memories. She came across a pencil drawing of a house that looked oddly familiar. She stood staring at the picture and then curiously asked, "Did you draw this?"

Cash joined her in front of the black-framed picture and smiled. "That is my childhood home. Some of my best memories were in that house. My parents built it; my mother wanted something bigger, so they sold it when I was 15 to a couple with two younger kids, I believe. I loved that house, and my dad had a drawing made, framed, and gave it to me this past Christmas," he said, smiling at the memory.

Cami continued to stare at the oddly familiar home. "Where is this, Cash? Is this in Atlanta?" she asked.

He furrowed his brow, struck by her curiosity. "Yes, it's on the Northside of Atlanta, Janie Drive," he said.

Cami's mouth dropped open, shocked by the revelation. "1708 Janie Drive?!"

Cash laughed, surprised by her knowledge of his childhood home. "Yes, how the fuck did you know that?"

Cami grinned, her eyes widening in disbelief. She shook her head, leaving Cash even more curious. "What is it, Cami? How did you know that? You are freaking me out."

Cami turned to look at the picture again and revealed, "Cash, that is also my childhood home. My parents bought that house when I was 10. I remember the day we moved in. There was this really cute 15-year-old boy with black wavy hair and a pink polo shirt. He was loading a box into a car while his parents handed off the extra keys."

She pointed to the last window in the picture. "That was my room. I lived there until I was 18 and went back a few times after my first divorce."

Cash was shocked. "Holy shit, I remember that day like it was yesterday. I did not want to leave that house. I remember thinking while loading my albums in the back of the car, who would have my room? Wow, you have got to be kidding me."

The pair laughed at the coincidence, their laughter filling the room before settling into a comfortable silence. In that quiet moment, an instant connection sparked between them. Cash placed his beer down on the table and slowly moved his hand behind the nape of Cami's neck, drawing her closer as he began kissing her. The passion was instantaneous, different from anything Cami had ever felt before.

As their kiss deepened, Cami started to unbutton Cash's shirt, her fingers trembling with anticipation. Meanwhile, Cash's hands moved with urgency, furiously unzipping the back of her dress. The air around them crackled with electricity, leaving no question about what was about to ensue.

Cash picked Cami up, carrying her to the bed without breaking their kiss. He gently laid her naked body down, his eyes never leaving hers as he stood at the end of the bed, undressing.

In a moment of clarity, Cami asked, "Cash, is this too soon?" Cash laughed at the question, "No, we are grown, and the days of playing hard to get are long gone, Ms. Leone, and we have practically known each other since you were 10."

Cash then laid himself on top of her, caressing her cheeks, and moved her hair away from her face as he entered her body, slowly making love to her.

The couple made love into the night, catching glimpses of themselves in a large, full-length mirror that sat against the wall. Cami stared at Cash in the mirror while he made love to her from behind, gently pulling at her hair and massaging her waist. The sounds of their lovemaking echoed into the night until they found themselves curled up in the bed, holding on to each other. Two lonely people with a common bond from their childhood fit together like a puzzle.

Cash nestled his face in Cami's hair as they lay in the darkness. "I think we even have the same house smell," Cash mumbled.

Cami burst into laughter. "What do you mean? Cash began to explain, "You know when you live in a house, and the smell of the house sticks to you, like certain shampoos and detergents?" "Come on now, unless you wash your hair with expensive salon shampoo, we do not have the same smell," she said sarcastically.

"Camille, my mother was a hairdresser. Of course, I wash my hair with expensive old lady salon shampoo," Cash replied

Cami quickly turned and propped herself on Cash's chest. "Are you serious?" she asked.

Cash started to laugh. "Paul Mitchell shampoo," he answered.

Cash rubbed Cami's head and stared at the ceiling, lost in thought. Cami noticed his distraction, "What's wrong?"

Cash paused but then had to ask, "So, do you still have feelings for Beau? And who is your ex?"

Cami felt uncomfortable but knew she had to address it. She started to get up when Cash tugged at her arm. "Wait, don't leave. We don't have to talk about it."

Cami found Cash's shirt and wrapped it around her, feeling the security of the clothing. She plopped back down on the bed, preparing herself for the dreaded conversation. "No, it's fine. As I told you earlier, Beau and I dated briefly for about eight or nine months. Yes, I was in love with him, or at least I thought I was. He was so genuine and kind when I was in a very bad place in my life. I hurt him, I lied to him, and I left him. Thankfully, because he has such a kind heart, we are friends now. No, I don't have feelings like that anymore. Sure, I care for him, but not romantically. That's about the gist of it. But Cash, I'm going to be honest: my past is the past. It's painful, and it's behind me. I just want to look forward."

Cash placed his arms behind his head and stared at Cami in awe of her beauty and kind heart. "I wish I could put my past behind me, but this ex of mine is something else. She is very hard to deal with... and my children."

Cash paused, and Cami could see the hurt in his eyes. "Do you see your children?" she asked.

Cash got up and walked confidently, naked, to the kitchen nestled in the center of the studio apartment. He grabbed a beer and bluntly stated, "Rarely, it's a fight. I'll try to keep you out of it if you'll have me. It's costing me a lot of money and stress. That's where all these gray hairs and crow's feet come from."

Cami got up and walked toward Cash, her eyes filled with compassion. "I think your salt and pepper hair and crow's feet are very sexy," she said, gently swiping at the small gray hairs around his face. She then reassured him, "I'm here for it, Cash."

Cash quickly picked Cami up and positioned her on the counter. "Thank you, but I really want to keep you out of it. I want you to hang out with me, and I'm worried that one day of dealing with that family, you may run back to Miami," Cash said, kissing her neck and chest, cupping her breast in his hands.

Cami chuckled at the thought of Miami. "I will never run back to Miami."

Cash placed both of his hands on Cami's face. "Never say never."

Cami smiled as she placed her lips on his and quietly repeated, "Never."

Chapter 15

Six Months Later

11:00 AM

Cami and Cash were inseparable, spending every free moment together. They found solace at Cami's place, nestled in a more secluded area of Atlanta. The house was surrounded by a small pond and a couple of acres of land, offering a peaceful retreat. They often took long walks in the woods, picking blackberries, a cherished memory from Cami's childhood with her cousins, and making love under the moonlight.

Cami set up a small studio for Cash in her three-story A-frame home, allowing him to work while staying close to her. She spent hours with him in the studio on the bottom floor, offering advice and even trying her hand at making music. Cash loved that she showed interest in his work, appreciated the late-night shoulder rubs, and reveled in the feeling of being truly loved.

One morning, Cami's phone rang, and her eyes lit up when she saw it was Cash. "Hello, darling," she said in her perfect southern drawl, a stark contrast to her attempts at speaking Spanish with Mateo.

"Hello, sweetheart, my beautiful princess," Cash replied endearingly. Cami smiled at his greeting.

"I need to go into the REAL studio this morning, and I have a meeting with my attorney about the divorce. I think he's trying to screw me. I swear these crazy people have paid him off. I need to make a decision; I really want to fire him and get another lawyer," Cash remarked, a disappointed tone in his voice.

Cami's eyes lit up, thinking of her lawyer in Florida, Ashley Strong. "Cash, I have a fantastic lawyer in Florida. I'm not sure about the laws regarding out-of-state jurisdiction, but I can call her. She represented me in a few things; she's a real bulldog for the truth," she said excitedly.

Curious, Cash asked, "Like what? What did she represent you in?"

Cami paused, not expecting the question, and felt her heart flutter. She quickly answered, "Just some business matters, but I've seen her in action on more serious cases, not mine, of course."

"I'll let you know this afternoon. If he doesn't give me any good news today, then we'll call her. I need a really good one. I need this family out of my life and a relationship with my children. I can't wait for you to meet them, princess."

"Me neither, sweetheart. We'll work this out, I promise," Cami replied, her voice filled with determination and love.

Cami hesitantly picked up the phone, trying to ignore the sick feeling of involving anyone from her past with Cash. Ultimately, she decided to call Ashley Strong's office without consulting Cash. She dialed the number, her heart racing slightly.

"Good afternoon, Young and Strong Law Firm. How can I help you?" answered a young secretary with a bright, professional tone.

Cami didn't recognize the voice. "Hello, is Ashley Strong available?" she asked, trying to keep her voice steady.

The woman quickly responded, "She has someone in her office at the moment. Can I please let her know who is calling?"

"Yes, ma'am. This is Camille Leone," Cami replied, hoping Ashley would remember her and respond quickly.

11:30 AM

Ashley Strong leaned over her oversized mahogany desk in her office, situated in a downtown high-rise in Miami. The office, surrounded by glass walls, offered a picturesque view of the cityscape. As she flipped through the documents her client was waiting to sign, her office phone buzzed. Agitated by the interruption from her recently hired, inexperienced secretary, she quickly answered, "Yes, Rachel, I am with someone. What is it?" Her aggravation was palpable.

"I apologize, Ms. Strong. You have a phone call, and I wasn't sure if you wanted to take it," Rachel said nervously.

"Well, Rachel, that's what you are there for—to take a message when I am with my clients. A very important client, by the way," Ashley stated firmly.

"Okay, I'll let Ms. Leone know that you will call her back," Rachel replied, still sounding unsure.

Ashley lifted her glasses to the top of her head, shocked by the name she hadn't heard in more than a year. "Wait, Rachel, is that Camille Leone?"

"Yes, ma'am," Rachel confirmed, her voice still nervous.

Ashley slowly placed her glasses on her desk and sat back in her plush leather chair. "Rachel, place her on hold and tell her I'll be right with her."

"Yes, ma'am," Rachel responded, pleased that she seemed to have done something right.

Ashley looked across the desk at the man waiting to sign his papers. His complacent demeanor had now turned to curiosity. Ashley knew that Mateo would want every detail of the conversation after hearing Camille's name. The air in the office grew tense with unspoken questions as the past seemed to catch up with the present at that moment.

Ashley picked up the phone, careful to hold it against her ear so as not to break any attorney-client privilege. "Camille, how are you? It's been a while. How can I help you?" she greeted warmly.

"Hi Ashley, I'm actually doing wonderful. How are you?" Camille responded.

"Doing well, just very busy. You know Miami is not lacking in divorce, crime, or personal injury," Ashley replied wittily.

Camille scoffed. "You got that right," she said.

"So, how can I help you?" Ashley asked, leaning back in her chair. Camille paused, slowly losing her nerve, then decided to just ask.

"Well, first and foremost, I want this to stay between us. Of course, I don't need to say it, but I know you have a long-standing relationship with Mateo, and I would like my life to remain private from him."

Ashley snickered, feeling somewhat offended by the implication that she might break her attorney-client privilege but also sensing a pang of guilt as she glanced at Mateo, knowing he would be curious about the call. "Camille, I have vowed to protect that privilege. Our business stays between us," Ashley assured her.

"Well, there is no business to protect yet. I just need to ask if you can represent someone in Georgia in a very nasty contested divorce, even though you are a Florida attorney. This man really needs a good divorce lawyer, and you are the best I know of," Camille said.

"Oh, so this is not a matter concerning you, but a friend of yours?" Ashley asked.

"Yes, his name is Cash Davidson. He's a music producer here in Atlanta. He's thinking about firing his attorney and is afraid of wasting money on another one if he can't get the results he needs," Camille explained.

Ashley scribbled the name on a piece of paper. Mateo, sitting stone-faced, glanced at the paper and took a mental note of the name. "Camille, you know this could be very costly. There is an application process, and I'll need to partner with one of my colleagues in Georgia, Richard Young. He's a great lawyer and well-respected. I'm not going to get into the details now, but I will certainly look into it and shoot you an email," Ashley stated.

"Perfect, I'm looking forward to hearing from you. I don't believe money will be an issue; just don't knock his head off. Maybe he will get a friendly discount," Camille chuckled.

"We can work something out. Is there anything else?" Ashley asked.

There was a long silence. Camille thought about asking about Mateo, the urge tugging at her. "Yeah, there is one more thing; you know what, never mind. Have a good day, Ashley. We'll talk soon," Camille said politely and ended the call.

Ashley hung up the phone and stared at Mateo, bracing for the interrogation. He surprised her by asking only one question. "How did she sound? Happy?" Mateo asked.

Ashley looked at Mateo with compassion. She knew the love he had for Camille was genuine, and she had watched him settle with Esme for the sake of his son Victor. Despite his broken spirit, Mateo remained strong, handsome, and a desired man in the community despite his transgressions and lust for women.

"She actually sounded really good, happy. It appears a friend of hers needs some help, and no, I will not discuss it with you. Now, let's finish this paperwork and legitimize Victor. This should be a happy day for you, Mateo. Don't spend it thinking about the past," Ashley said bluntly.

Mateo gave her a half smile and leaned in to sign the paperwork. However, the faint sound of Camille's voice over the receiver had brought back so many memories and suppressed feelings. He dropped the pen on the paper, took a deep breath, and walked out, repeating Cash Davidson's name in his head over and over until he made it to his car.

Sitting in the parking lot, Mateo scrolled through his phone for any information about Cash. He was surprised to see that Cash was a bit older and very mature-looking. He appeared happy in all his photos on the internet, a picture of happiness with his young wife and two children. "Wonder who ruined that marriage," he thought to himself.

Continuing his search, he came across a picture of Cash and Beau at a music festival in Canada. Mateo stared at the picture, unable to understand the connection. "Is she with Beau or his producer? Could he be just a friend of Beau's, and Camille was helping him?" he muttered, his curiosity piqued. The thought of her being happy with someone else gnawed at his soul. Mateo knew he had to leave it alone, but his heart wouldn't let him.

"Leave it alone," he repeated to himself as he drove home. Yet, the urgency to know more took over. Stopping at a red light, he banged on the steering wheel, frustrated with himself. Then, with a swift U-turn, he headed back to downtown Miami. He was going to visit a longtime friend who he knew could get him more answers.

****

Cami strolled through the meat department of the supermarket, preparing to cook a homemade meal to serve Cash over candlelight, hoping to give him the good news of speaking with Ashley Strong. She grabbed two ribeyes, some baked potatoes, and fresh broccoli. Cash was a meat-and-potatoes man who enjoyed the occasional vegetable. Cami laughed as she looked at her shopping cart. "I went from Pablo Escobar to John Wayne," she said to herself.

She walked to the wine aisle, feeling the freedom to choose as many bottles as she wanted. She and Cash enjoyed drinking together, a luxury she hadn't had with Mateo. Cami chose a nice bottle of Merlot and a six-pack of beer for Cash. As she was checking out, her phone rang.

"Hi, Mom!" Gabriella said excitedly.

"Hi, sweetheart! How are you? I sure miss you. What are you doing?" Cami asked.

Gabriella didn't hesitate. "Mom, I'm so excited! I got this really great job."

"Really? A new job?, I thought you loved your marketing job?" Cami asked.

"I do, Mom, but I wanted to do something different and applied for this one, not really expecting to get it. But, Mom, I need to tell you something," Gabriella said cautiously.

"Oh my God, Gabriella, are you pregnant?" Cami asked in a panic.

Gabriella started to laugh. "No, Mama. But I am kind of nervous about telling you this, so I'm just going to say it. The job is in Italy."

"Italy!" Camille screamed as she grabbed her groceries and headed out the door of the supermarket.

"Yes, Mama, Italy. You know we have dual citizenship, so I thought, why not? I speak fluent Italian, and you know I love to travel. I thought maybe you and I could fly over for a visit. We can visit a few vineyards, take a nice girls' trip, and get familiar with where I'll be living," Gabriella said.

Camille's heart swelled with pride. "Oh my God, Gabby, this is amazing! What are you going to do over there?" she inquired excitedly.

"Teach English," Gabriella stated confidently.

"Teaching? How are you going to do that? You don't have a teaching degree," Cami asked, her eyebrows raised in surprise.

"I am taking a bridge program and will start next school year," Gabriella explained, her excitement palpable.

"Oh God, does your Nonna know? You should have been more scared to tell her than me," Cami remarked with a laugh.

"I know, right? Well, anyway, Mom, I have to run. Let's have dinner soon. I know you and Cash are hot and heavy now—I need details!" Gabriella laughed, her eyes sparkling with curiosity.

"Yes, honey, let's do that. I think he may be the one," Cami said, shocked at her own revelation.

"Really, Mom?" Gabriella asked, equally surprised.

"Yes, I think so. Anyway, I have to get these groceries home. I'm cooking for Cash tonight. I've yet to show off my real culinary skills, so I need to go. I love you."

"Love you, Mommy, and I am very happy for you," Gabriella said in a sweet, childlike voice.

Chapter 16

Mateo confidently walked through the lobby of a posh office building in downtown Miami, his footsteps echoing off the polished marble floors. He greeted the receptionist with a warm smile.

"Good afternoon, Mr. Vega," the young girl greeted flirtatiously. Mateo returned her smile but didn't break stride. He swung open the doors to the music studio, where he found Fernando Pena standing in the background, listening intently to his latest artist.

Surprised to see Mateo, Fernando looked up, perplexed. "Mateo, what are you doing here? Did we have a meeting I wasn't aware of?"

"No, no, no, señor. I was just stopping by to see your latest project," Mateo replied.

"Absolutely, please do. This is my latest discovery—a blend of Latin rap, southern hip hop, and reggaeton. It's the hottest thing hitting the airwaves." Fernando gestured toward the artist in the recording booth, a young Hispanic male pouring his heart into a song of love and desire, with a talented rapper joining in on the chorus in English. The blend of languages and styles was mesmerizing.

"Brilliant," Fernando complimented the artists. "Let's take a break. We'll resume in an hour or so." He looked at Mateo knowingly, sensing there was more to this visit. "Let's step into my office," Fernando suggested, gesturing for Mateo to follow.

The two men entered Fernando's office, a space filled with memorabilia and awards. They sat down, engaging in small talk about their children before Mateo broached the topic he was really interested in.

"How did you get started in this business, Fernando?" Mateo asked.

Fernando leaned back in his chair, his brow furrowing slightly as he considered the question. "Well, as you know, Mateo, I own several clubs here in Miami and Atlanta where I have booked local talent to showcase their music, so I thought instead of just giving them a stage to perform, why not produce them? It's been very lucrative, especially with the talent we have here in Miami and Atlanta."

Mateo hesitated for a moment before asking, "Atlanta, too?"

"Yes, Atlanta. I work with several artists out of Atlanta and often reserve local studios to hear fresh talent," Fernando explained.

"How can I get into this business? I'm curious. I love the Latin style with some American collaboration. I know there are plenty of new artists out there riding this new wave," Mateo stated.

Fernando looked at Mateo curiously, sensing there was more behind his question but not pressing the issue. "I tell you what, Mateo. Why don't you work with me on some new talent, learn the business, and see if you like it? We both know you've made every project I've ever worked on turn into gold. Why not add a few gold records to the list?" Fernando suggested with a hint of sarcasm.

Mateo smirked, a sly grin spreading across his face. "That sounds perfect. When can I start?" he asked.

Fernando checked his schedule. "I'll be checking out a new artist in Atlanta in a couple of weeks. If you want to tag along," he offered.

"Perfect. Let me know the exact dates. I'll have my secretary book us a flight. We'll make a stay of it," Mateo said, excitement in his voice.

As they shook hands, Mateo felt a surge of satisfaction. His plan was taking shape.

****

Cami stood in her cozy kitchen on the second floor of her modest home, whipping up homemade mashed potatoes and washing broccoli sprouts. The scent of marinated steaks filled the air as she set them out, preparing the grill on the deck.

She paused for a moment, looking out over the deck at the small pond. The sun was setting over the trees, casting a warm, golden glow, while a flock of geese flew overhead in a perfect V formation. The peace she felt in her soul was indescribable.

Suddenly, Cash startled her, breaking her gaze from the sky. "Hello, darling," he said, kissing her neck lightly. A warm smile lit up her face as she turned around for a kiss.

"What are you doing here so early? I was going to surprise you with dinner," Cami questioned.

Cash leaned in for another kiss, pecking her lips repeatedly. "I couldn't wait to see you. I want to ravish you," he said, moving to her neck and sliding his hands up her shirt.

"Sweetheart, I'm cooking you a nice dinner. You can ravish me afterward. I have everything ready; I just need to put the steaks on the grill. They're in the refrigerator waiting for me," Cami said as she tried to slip through his arms.

"No, I want you now. Those steaks aren't going anywhere; they're dead," Cash said determinedly.

Cami looked at him, speechless. His sexiness, his odd sense of humor, and the connection they both had were irresistible. They fell into a passionate kiss, walking through the sliding glass doors toward the stairs.

Cash couldn't wait any longer, lifting her skirt and gently placing her on the stairs, kissing her ankles and licking her inner thighs. He unbuttoned his pants in a fury and began making love to her on the stairwell. It was only minutes before the two exploded in ecstasy, laughing at their quick encounter.

Cash pushed himself up, pecking Cami on the lips. "Now I'm starving. Just call me three-minute-man," he said jokingly.

Cami laughed at his joke. "Yeah, honey, that was pretty quick, but I am satisfied," she said, laughing as she pulled her skirt down and headed to the sink to wash her hands.

"There's more where that came from," Cash yelled from the bedroom, unwinding and starting the shower after the long day's work.

Cami shook her head and chuckled, grabbing the steaks and placing them on the grill.

****

Setting the table with an elegant touch and lighting each candle, Cami and Cash sat on the deck of the three-story A-frame home, enjoying the impeccable meal Cami had prepared. The evening air was crisp, and the soft glow of the candles cast a warm, intimate light over them.

"Do you like it?" she asked, watching Cash devour his dinner.

"God, yes, your cooking is amazing, sweetheart. I haven't had cooking like this in ages," he replied, taking a swig of his beer.

"Really? Your ex-wife, or wife should I say, didn't cook?" Cami inquired.

Cash looked at Cami over the candlelight and chuckled. "Not my wife, and oh, she cooked. Was it good? No, but she cooked. Put it this way, I've eaten so many salmon patties that the thought of one makes me choke," Cash said, making a gagging sound.

Cami laughed, then hesitated. "Speaking of, I spoke with Ashley Strong, the lawyer I was telling you about in Miami. She's going to check on some things and see if she can represent you. She has a partner who works here in Atlanta. He can actually litigate the case, from what I understand, and she could help him with it. She's the best, and maybe we can finally close the book on all this nonsense," Cami said compassionately.

Cash picked up his beer, appearing a bit aggravated. "Cami, I really don't want you involved in this. I'm actually to the point where I'm going to give her what she wants and hope that my kids miss me enough to want to see me. This is so much more complicated than you can imagine. I don't know if I want to keep doing this financially. These people are about the win, and they don't play fair. They will say or do anything to make me look bad, even at the expense of my children. I don't want to put my kids through that," Cash said, exhausted.

Cami became frustrated. "Cash, you have to get this over with. You can't let these people continue to treat you like this. This attorney you have will continue to bleed you dry with little to no results. I trust Ashley to get the job done. And Cash, listen to me, these people are not invincible. Why are you so afraid of them?" she asked with urgency.

"I'm not afraid of them. I fear what they are going to do to my children. They are ruthless, Camille," Cash said with frustration.

Cami crossed her arms. "Well, so am I. Do you want to give up and let your children think you never fought for them? I've been divorced; I have never had an issue with letting my children know that their father loved them despite our differences. This is just fucking insane to me," she said firmly.

She then got up from the table, grabbed both dinner plates, and slung them into the sink with a clatter. Cash followed behind her. "Hey, this is exactly why I did not want you involved. Here we are, fighting. That's what this family does—if they ever infiltrate your life, this is what happens, pure fucking chaos. I told you to stay the fuck out of it!" Cash screamed.

Cami was stunned; Cash had never raised his voice or spoken to her in that manner. She had never seen him angry. He knew he scared her and approached her cautiously. "Camille, I am so sorry," he said lovingly.

Cami wiped a tear from her cheek and went to her bedroom, where she lay on her bed, confused by what she had done and questioning her own intentions. Cash walked to his studio, shutting the door behind him, and began working on his music, angry with himself for allowing his temper to get the best of him.

Cami lay in her bed listening to the faint beats of the music. After calming down, she cautiously walked to the studio she had so perfectly created for Cash in her home. She stood in the doorway, staring at him as he put one beat together after another, sampling each one and feeling the frustrations of not being able to get it right when he sensed her presence behind him.

"Come here, beautiful," he said. Cami slowly walked to the man she was so fond of and immensely desired. A man she had so much in common with, five years her senior, a shared past, experienced, and so genuine and loving. It was as if the universe had reconnected them. She straddled him in the chair, and he kissed her body slowly, reminding her of his gentle nature with every touch. She started to move her hips back and forth and began to make love to him in the chair.

"Is this make-up sex?" Cash whispered in her ear. Cami smiled and slowly stuck her tongue in his ear. Cash took a deep breath, feeling his stomach give way to butterflies as they made passionate love for hours.

Cami and Cash woke the next morning on the brown leather couch, wrapped in a soft fleece blanket. Cash rubbed her hair and, in a sweet voice, whispered, "Good morning," squeezing her tightly, thankful she was there. He felt an urgency to let her know how he felt.

"Camille, I am so in love with you. Please, princess, I don't want to fight like that again," Cash said urgently and effortlessly.

"In love?" Camille repeated, perplexed. The word had not come up, and with Cash's divorce still looming, love was not a subject they had approached. She turned to look Cash in the eyes.

"Yes, in love, Cami. I am deeply in love with you," he said. Cami studied his eyes; they were sincere, but love scared her. Total commitment scared her. She swallowed the lump in her throat, wanting to reciprocate but terrified to jump back into this thing called love. Love had not been her friend in the past.

"Cash, I don't know what to say," Cami whispered.

Cash stared at her. "I know you feel this too; this feels like home, you feel like home, Camille. I have never felt more comfortable and alive with a woman. There was nothing there with my ex. Sure, I cared for her at some point, but not like this. Never like this. Why are you afraid of this? Is it Beau?" Cash questioned.

Cami laughed. "Beau? No, Beau and I are friends. That has been over for a very long time," she stated. Then she realized she had never spoken of her relationship with Mateo. She had never shared her past with Cash, only bits and pieces. They had been so wrapped up in his divorce and each other, vowing never to speak of him, making him nonexistent in her life. Cash truly knew nothing about her; the pain she had felt when she lost Mateo and the legal issues in Miami were all dark secrets she had locked away.

Cami bit her lip, trying to find the words, but they continued to escape her. Cash slowly got up and started to get dressed. He felt rejected.

"Where are you going?" Cami mustered.

"I am going home, Cami. I think we need a break. I have a lot going on. I need to go into the studio more and focus on this divorce," Cash stated bluntly as he slipped on his leather shoes.

Cami could feel her panic rising. "Cash, I am sorry. I am just shocked. I do care for you, and you do feel like home to me," Cami begged.

Cash snickered at her words. "Care for me? Is that what you call it? Cami, I know nothing about you other than you dated a rapper five years younger than you. You've been married twice, maybe three times, but that subject is taboo, so we don't discuss that. You lived in my childhood home, which blows my fucking mind, by the way, and your favorite color is yellow. That's it, that's all I know," Cash belted out.

Cami's frustration was palpable. "What else do you need to know, Cash? I mean, that's about it. You summed it up. There is nothing interesting about me," Cami retorted.

Cash sighed, looking at her with a mix of sadness and frustration. "It's not about interesting, Cami. It's about knowing you, understanding you. I want to share my life with you, but I feel like you're holding back."

Cami looked away, tears welling in her eyes. She had never felt this vulnerable. "I've been hurt before, Cash. Deeply. My ex was... he was everything to me, and when I lost him, I lost a part of myself. And losing my business in Miami…. it's all just too much. I wanted to leave it behind, start fresh with you."

Cash softened, walking over to her. "I understand, Cami. But if we're going to be together, really be together, I need to know all of you. Not just the parts you think are safe to share." Cash added firmly before stepping away from her.

"Cash…." Cami whispered desperately but Cash wasn't having any of it. It was clear that she wasn't ready to share anything with him despite him trying his best to make her feel secure.

Sighing, he grabbed some bags and walked to the door. He stopped midway and turned to Cami, "Oh, there is a lot about you I don't know, Camille. There are seven entire years of your life I know nothing about, and somewhere in between, you dated Beau. I happen to be his producer. You know, Cami, you are a beautiful, kind, intelligent, and sweet woman, but he warned me about you. He said you are trouble for the heart— a treacherous butterfly, like that tattoo inked on your body, wreaking havoc on a man's heart as you float from man to man, like flowers in a field, making them fall in love with you only to leave them damaged and wilted. Just like that song you love to belt out in Spanish, which I hate, just so you know. Yeah, there is something you're hanging on to, and I just can't pinpoint what it is. You know what? I am going to quit trying. So when you're ready to let me in and tell me who you are and why the word 'love' is so hard for you to reciprocate, let me know," Cash hurled at her.

Cami could feel her heart race, her feelings crushed like a child by a schoolyard bully. She picked herself up off the couch, her eyes welling with tears, her head shaking in agreement. Cash waited for her to respond, but Cami could not find her voice. Cash scoffed, turning to give her one more chance, then reluctantly walked out the door.

The room felt colder without him, an empty space lingering where his presence had been. Cami's mind swirled with memories and regrets, her hands trembling as she wiped away the tears streaming down her cheeks.

Chapter 17

Two Weeks Later

Cami called Julia, seeking sound advice on matters of the heart. Julia had never been one to hold back her opinions, and Cami needed an honest one right now. Cash and Cami, both headstrong, had refused to contact each other during their standoff. Cami dialed Julia's number, looking for direction.

"Hey girl, what are you doing?" Cami asked.

In true Julia fashion, she quickly responded with her troubles for the day. "Trying to break up these fucking cats. You know how territorial they are. Now, I have a vet bill I cannot afford. I should have let those little fuckers fight it out to the death; it would save me on food every month. One less mouth to feed," Julia said, frustrated.

"That's why I have one cat. I couldn't imagine having two. This little gray one is a lot by herself. But anyway, speaking of catfights, Cash and I haven't spoken in two weeks," Cami said, disappointed.

Julia's curiosity was evident. "Oh God, why not? I really liked him too. He seemed so normal and legal," she said sarcastically.

"Julia, seriously, I don't know what to do. We have so much in common. We literally grew up in the same house, in the same bedroom. You can't tell me that's not universal stardust coming together. We get along so well, other than these past two weeks. Things have just been so strange," Cami explained.

"So what's the problem? I'm sure he's in love with you like the rest of them. Did he get his feelings hurt because you won't fully commit?" Julia asked knowingly.

"Dammit, Julia, how do you know this shit? Do you have a bug in my house?" Cami asked, aggravated.

"No, bitch, I know you. Since Mateo, you have this hard, cold shell around you. This 'I'm independent and need no one, let me take care of you because I don't want anyone taking care of me' attitude. Cami, you don't see this in yourself, but others have. You should talk to someone about Mateo and what happened in Miami. For fuck's sake, you almost went to jail, lost your business, found out about a love child, lost your money, and had to rebuild your life. Not to mention you went through a few dangerous men like old winter clothes," Julia blasted.

"Julia, it was not that many men. Did I make some bad decisions? Sure, but I was hurt. There's no point in discussing Mateo. Cash does not need to know any of that. As far as I'm concerned, that part of my life never happened," Cami stated.

"But it did happen, Cami. And I dare say you haven't seen the last of him," Julia said with concern.

"Mateo is long gone, Julia. It's been close to two years now. He's settled with Esme, and anyway, I don't want to speak on it again. What do I do about Cash? He's angry because he says he doesn't know me, that I don't let him in, and I'm a mystery...... Beau warned him about me, and then, of course, the whole tattoo analogy came into play. I should have never gotten this tattoo. It's cursed me with men. It's like a love-hate relationship I have with all of them. I'm going to have this damn thing covered up or removed," Cami said with displeasure.

"Cami, listen to me. Make the first move. Call or text him, tell him you two need to talk, and tell him everything. He needs to know. It's not like you can't google that shit. If he ever found out your last name was Vega, it'd be a wrap. It's on the internet," Julia said amusingly.

"You're right. He'll either accept me and my past, or he won't. And if he won't, I'll just keep this wall stacked a little higher for the next one," Cami said confidently.

"Stop it, Cami. Call the man, tell him y'all need to talk, and just get it out in the open. Now, I am going to smoke a joint, have a Coke, watch some Netflix, and referee two feral cats. Let me know how it goes. I love you," Julia said.

"Okay, I will. Love you too," Cami said sheepishly and hung up the phone.

****

Mateo strolled through his Miami South Beach penthouse, a white towel wrapped tightly around his waist. Esme sat on the couch with Victor, watching cartoons, when she noticed Mateo opening a large suitcase on the bed and packing. Her curiosity piqued.

"Where are you going, Mateo?" Esme asked, handing Victor a juice cup.

Mateo continued to meticulously fold his clothes, glancing at the two of them through the bedroom door. Feeling a tinge of guilt, he answered, "I have a business trip planned with

Fernando. I'll be gone for about a week or so. We're leaving in a couple of days.

Esme, never fully trusting Mateo, began to probe further. "But where, darling?" she questioned.

"California, Esme. We're going to meet a new artist and see what he's made of. He's done really well on social media and this new platform called TikTok. We have to get to this artist before someone else does," Mateo explained.

To avoid more of Esme's questioning, Mateo walked over and gave her a gentle kiss, reassuring her of his devotion. Esme smiled, ignoring the gut feeling that Camille Leone was once again coursing through her lover's veins. Mateo picked up the phone and called his secretary, speaking in his native tongue, to confirm his flight to Atlanta International Airport. He dared not let Esme know he was flying to Atlanta, Cami's hometown, or give her any reason to raise suspicion among his uncle Aldo and mother.

Esme followed him to the bedroom, wrapping her arms around his waist. "We are going to miss you so much, my love," she said, her way of reminding him that he was hers now. Esme started to feel more powerful as her relationship lengthened, using Victor as a pawn. Mateo knew that meeting with Ashley and legitimizing his son was a slow start to his methodical escape from Esme.

With Camille heavy on Mateo's mind, the thought of making love to Esme sickened him. He had been hyper-focused on Cami for weeks now, and his departure from Miami was just days away.

Mateo started to rub Esme's hands. "I am going to miss you too, my love and our little Mijo. But I will be back soon," Mateo said convincingly.

"Not soon enough," Esme replied as she ran her hand up his towel. Mateo could feel himself getting aroused but could hear Victor in the other room.

"Esme, do we really have time for this? Victor is in the other room. I just showered," Mateo said, his voice a mix of desire and concern.

Esme locked her eyes onto his as she started to rub him between his legs, slowly moving her hands up and down his shaft. "Victor is occupied with his cartoons; this will not take long. I promise."

She closed the door to the bathroom and dropped to her knees, placing her mouth around his penis, using the wetness of her mouth to ensure his orgasm was smooth and memorable.

Mateo exploded in ecstasy, only to be reminded that the woman between his legs was not the woman behind his eyes.

****

Cami opened the text screen and began her message to Cash, backing out several times. Cami felt angry with Cash. There was no sadness, just frustration.

"How dare he question me about my past? He doesn't have the slightest idea what my life has been like. Fuck this shit," Cami said to herself, throwing her phone down.

Pouring a glass of wine, she tried to think through her next attempt at communicating with Cash. Her phone rang. It was

Ashley Strong. Cami quickly answered, remembering the conversation she had with her the week before.

"Hello," Cami answered.

"Hello, Camille, this is Ashley. Listen, I have spoken with my partner Richard Young in Georgia, and we would be more than happy to meet with your friend and discuss representation," Ashley stated, excited to give Camille the news.

"Oh, wow, Ashley, that's awesome. I'll be sure to let him know and how to get in contact with you," Cami replied.

"Now, if he wants to make an appointment, have him call my secretary, Rachel. She will set something up through Zoom, and we can discuss his case," Ashley assured.

"Great, that sounds wonderful, Ashley. I'll let him know as soon as possible. Thanks, we will talk soon," Cami said and ended the call. "Fuck, I totally forgot about that. I have to call him or text now," she said to herself as she continued her rant, but felt relieved she had a reason to reach out.

"You know I'm just trying to help, and this ungrateful… stop it, Camille Leone," she said to herself, continuing her one-sided conversation as she picked up the phone and started to text Cash, *"Hi, do you think we could meet for coffee and talk?"*

****

Cash and Beau sat in the studio, tying up some loose ends before The MIXX moved out west. Beau could see the familiar look on Cash's face. Cash's focus was somewhere else. Beau knew the feeling all too well but dared not address it directly. Instead, he asked casually, "Hey man, you ok?"

Cash looked over at Beau with a curious look. "Yeah, man, I'm good. Why you ask?" Cash questioned.

"Man, I can see that shit all over your face. You're not focused; your mind is on another planet," Beau observed compassionately.

Cash shook his head. "It's just this divorce, Camille, and not to mention I'm losing two of my best artists to the West Coast," Cash said, gesturing toward Beau.

"Man, this ain't got shit to do with me and Salty going to California. That look on your face is because that pussy got you fucked up. I tried to warn you," Beau said bluntly.

Cash furrowed his brow, curious about Beau's remarks. "What do you mean? Camille? Is that who you're referring to?" he asked.

"Unless you're fucking more than one bitch, yeah, that's exactly who I'm referring to," Beau stated knowingly.

Cash became quiet and then couldn't contain his curiosity any longer. "Man, tell me about her. She's so fucking elusive. Right when I think we are in love and moving forward, she can't commit. Why is that? What did she do to you so I can understand this better?" Cash asked, his hurt obvious.

Beau drew in his breath, careful not to say too much as not to break his promise to Camille. "Well, at least she's NOT committing to you. Try thinking you're committed, and you come home, and the bitch is a different person. No breakup and makeup shit, no kind of conversation about working this shit out. Just, 'I'm sorry, I'm leaving you.' Shit was fucked up, man. I'm telling you, be careful with her. She is a sweet woman;

she is a good woman, but she is also indecisive and flighty as fuck—from the drive-through at McDonald's to your heart. That woman doesn't know what she wants half the time," Beau stated plainly.

"But why? What happened to her? I know she was married, had a short stay in Miami, and came back broke, working her way back to the top, or at least even from what I can tell. I know she is a hard worker; she just has this coldness about her, a wall that you cannot penetrate. I feel like I am in love with her and told her so. She never responded back, just speechless," Cash recalled, feeling heartbroken.

"Man, that's actually not a bad thing. At least she's not drawing you into that web. She's giving you a chance to save yourself. It probably means she does love you and doesn't want to hurt you," Beau said.

"Did something happen in Miami that I need to know about?" Cash asked.

Beau lit his cigarette, staring at Cash intently, wanting so badly to tell his friend about Mateo, but kept his promise to Camille. "Man, that's something you will have to talk to her about. I know nothing about her time in Miami," Beau said.

Cash shook his head and accepted his answer. "Speaking of Miami, I have two music producers flying in sometime this week or next. They're meeting with a few studios out here and have some artists they want to sample, so I really need to focus this week and forget this shit. Look, man, on another note, I want to wish you and Salty the best of luck in California. I know you guys are going to make it. Just don't forget about me," Cash said as the two men laughed and shared a hug.

"Naw, man, you know I'll keep in touch and give you all the credit where it's due," Beau said as he left the studio, leaving Cash in his thoughts.

Cash's phone vibrated in his pocket. He pulled it out to see it was Cami. He read the text and smirked with a hint of satisfaction that he held out long enough for her to text him. Maybe he would be the one to win her over. Cash left the text on read for more than 30 minutes before he responded and finally accepted her invitation for coffee.

Sure, where would you like to meet? Cash texted back.

Camille paced the kitchen, glancing at her phone several times, waiting for the text from Cash. When it finally came through, her heart was full and relieved that he was not going to ignore her or give her the silent treatment. Camille quickly began to respond but then deleted it, feeling she should make him wait as he did her.

She thought about a place. *How about Starbucks on Peachtree in Lenox Square around 1:00 tomorrow?* She sent the text with anticipation. She watched the bubbles quickly appear.

Ok, see you then." Cash typed back.

Cami responded with a heart emoji, to which Cash left her on read.

****

Cami woke the next morning and went through her routine, hoping coffee would ease some of the anxiety she was feeling. Her heart began to race, thinking about the conversation she would be having with Cash and the fear that the question of her past would come up.

She rehearsed her conversation over and over, trying to find a way to tell him about her troubled past. Camille took deep, long breaths, closing her eyes and seeing Mateo's face, replaying their life together and thinking of Cash and how wonderful he had been. They shared so many things in common, including their shared experiences growing up in the same home. This had to be fate, she thought to herself.

She called Julia one last time for advice. "Hey, what are you doing?" she asked in a panicked tone.

"Hey girl, what is wrong with you? You sound like you've been running a marathon. You okay?" Julia responded.

"No, Julia, I am having a panic attack, and I have no idea why," Cami said, her panic undeniable.

"Girl, calm down and tell me why. Is Mateo in town? You know that motherfucker can sniff you out from anywhere," Julia said sarcastically.

"No, Julia, this has nothing to do with Mateo. Well, it kind of does, but no, he is not here; at least, I don't think he is. Anyway, it's about Cash," she said, frustrated by her friend's sarcasm.

"Okay, okay, what's going on?" Julia asked with compassion.

"I'm going to meet Cash for coffee. We haven't spoken in almost two weeks. I am going to tell him about this new lawyer I want him to try, but I am so worried he is going to ask me about Mateo and Miami. I don't know if I should tell him," Cami said, panicking.

"Cami, we have been through this. Listen to me; tell him little pieces at a time. Tell him you two will talk about it in your own time. He doesn't even know Mateo's name, does he?" Julia asked quizzically.

"No, he doesn't know anything about Mateo. I just really like him, and then the love stuff comes up. I don't know if I should just dive in or let him go," Cami said.

Julia snickered. "Bitch, you better dive in. That's the most normal man I have ever seen you with. Just calm down, go pick out something to wear, and let it happen naturally. You will know what to do," Julia said.

Cami started to feel calmness rush over her at the sound advice given by her friend. "Okay, I will. I just feel uneasy for some reason," Cami said.

"Well, don't. Take care of business. I love you," Julia said.

"Love you too. I'll call you later," Cami said.

The two ladies ended their call, and Cami headed for the shower with an uneasy feeling still lingering in her chest.

Chapter 18

Four Hours Later

Mateo and Fernando touched down in Atlanta, brimming with excitement to meet their new artist and explore the local studios. Mateo grabbed his carry-on from first class, dragging the rolling luggage through the bustling airport. As they descended the escalator, they caught sight of a familiar face going up in the opposite direction. It was Beau Machado, accompanied by Salty.

For a brief moment, their eyes met; Beau smirked at Mateo and shook his head in disgust. "Was that Beau Machado?" Mateo asked Fernando.

"Ironically, yes, it was," Fernando replied knowingly. "I heard they were headed out to California with a new producer."

"Oh, really?" Mateo questioned, beginning to piece things together. He knew Cami wouldn't move out of the South. She must be dating Cash Davidson, as he suspected.

Mateo looked at Fernando with a curious expression. "So why don't we check out his old studio? His producer seems to have made them successful enough. I'm sure he'll have a state-of-the-art setup. Maybe he could help us out."

Fernando pondered the idea. "Sounds like a plan. What do we have to lose?" he stated, unaware of Mateo's ulterior motive to find Cami.

Mateo rolled his luggage out of the automatic doors of Hartsfield International and jumped into the back seat of a Rolls Royce with Fernando. Quietly staring out of the window all the way to his hotel, being in Atlanta made him feel closer to Camille with every passing moment.

****

Cash slowly pulled into valet parking at Lenox Square, stepping out of the vehicle with a casual grace. As he walked towards Starbucks, he spotted Camille entering the doors from a distance. She was breathtaking, and he felt a surge of arousal thinking about the way she made love to him so passionately. He discreetly adjusted himself, rubbing the crotch of his pants before swinging the doors open to see her situated in a cozy corner, flipping through a magazine.

"Hi," he greeted her, situating himself in a comfortable chair across from her.

"Hi," Cami responded sheepishly.

"Can I get you anything, or have you ordered?" he asked.

"No, I haven't ordered, but a matcha would be nice," Cami said.

Cash waved to the barista and placed their order for matcha and a Frappuccino. Turning back to Cami, he got straight to the point. "So, what is it you wanted to talk about?" he asked, trying to stay focused despite her intoxicating beauty.

"Well, first and foremost, I want to apologize for the other night," Cami began, her voice sincere. "When you said those words, I was shocked. Then, when you started bringing up my past, it freaked me out. I want to share things with you, but some things are still very fresh and raw. I will tell you everything in due time, but for now, I want to enjoy what we have. Cash, I do feel like I am falling in love with you, but I do not use those words lightly. I feel very connected to you with all the things we have in common from growing up."

Cash gazed into her eyes, searching for any hint of insincerity, remembering Beau's words. But her voice and beauty were captivating; he wanted her and only her. Cash reached across the table, lightly grasping her dainty hand, covering it with his own. "You know the way to a person's soul is through their eyes," Cash stated.

"Yes, I know that all too well and have heard that a thousand times," Cami said, looking down shyly.

"Don't look down; I want you to look at me when I say this," Cash said sternly.

Cami, shocked by his assertive tone yet turned on by his manliness, lifted her head and looked at Cash as he began to speak. "Camille, I am sorry if I brought up love too quickly. But it's only a word. I know you love me; I can feel it, I can see it in the things you do for me, I can taste it in the food you cook, and I can feel it in my heart. I don't need you to say it, and I am not going to ask you about your past. I will let you tell me when you're ready. I'm not going to judge you because whatever it is, it's over, and I can't stand the thought of another minute without you," Cash said lovingly, then lifted her hand to kiss it.

Cami felt relief wash over her body as she leaned in for a passionate kiss. They realized they were in public and pulled back when the barista stood in front of them. "I hate to interrupt, but here are your beverages, sir," she said.

Cash snickered and looked at Cami. "Let's get out of here; I want to take you somewhere."

"Absolutely," Cami said softly.

****

Camille and Cash buckled their seat belts and looked at each other with affection. "By the way, there is something else I wanted to speak with you about," Camille said with a grin on her face.

Cash cut his eyes toward her, a mix of concern and curiosity in his expression. "What is it?" he asked.

"Well, I spoke with my attorney from Miami, and she can take your case. She is the best. I really feel like you will get what you want and can finally put this entire situation behind you with this dysfunctional family you seem unable to shake. And maybe she can work out the custody issues too, so you can see your kids again," Camille said, hope filling her voice.

Cash placed his hand lovingly on her leg, rubbing her knee as he focused on the road ahead. "So, are you going to respond?" Camille asked.

"Yes, Princess, I really did not want you involved, but if you feel like this attorney can help, then I will fire the one I have and give her a shot," Cash stated hesitantly.

Camille clapped her hands together and smiled, leaning over to peck him on the cheek. "Now, where are we going?" she asked.

"You'll see," Cash replied, smiling, excitement bubbling about the day ahead.

****

Mateo and Fernando strolled through a cigar bar in Buckhead. Fernando, a lover of fresh cigars, ran the cigar across his nose and then offered it to Mateo to smell the freshness of the tobacco from Nicaragua. Mateo leaned in to smell the cigar, not impressed by the aroma, but kindly nodded in agreement, appeasing Fernando's passion for a good cigar. Inside, Mateo felt the pull of Cami's presence. His calm exterior gave Fernando no indication of his plan to see Camille, but his insides were raging with anticipation.

"What time will this artist be here?" Mateo asked curiously.

"Around six. I figured we would have a cigar and a nice bourbon while we wait," Fernando suggested.

Mateo smirked. "You know neither of those appeal to me. I'll have a water, and please, let's have a seat outside. It's nice out there, and I prefer not to be around the smoke," Mateo said.

Fernando nodded in agreement. "You know, Mateo, I've never understood your disdain for the finer things in life," he said jokingly.

"That's a matter of opinion, Fernando. The finer things in life, to me, are far different from your idea of finer things," Mateo replied knowingly.

Fernando gave Mateo a sly grin. "You mean money and women?" Fernando asked.

"Well, of course. Who wouldn't want money and beautiful women?" Mateo said bluntly.

Fernando took a seat in a black wrought-iron chair on the patio of the cigar bar. He snapped the end of his cigar and lit it, the flame casting a warm glow on his face as he took a puff of the finely wrapped tobacco. He gazed at Mateo through the rising smoke. "Speaking of women, how are you adjusting to your new life with Esme and Victor? I know all of that was a bit unexpected," Fernando paused, "and losing Camille, I'm sure that was tough," he added hesitantly.

Mateo looked away, his eyes following the bustling city streets. Memories of Camille and his ill-considered plan to see her surfaced, but he held his words back, denying his feelings. "Oh, Fernando, that has passed as far as I am concerned. I have my life with Esme and Victor now. My son is the most important person in my life, and no woman can change that," Mateo stated firmly.

Before Fernando could respond, a young, handsome, mixed-race Latino man approached their table. "Mr. Peña?" he asked. Both Mateo and Fernando, a bit startled by his early appearance, stood up. "Yes, you must be Manny T?" Fernando inquired. The young man smiled and extended his hand. "Yes, but for professional purposes, please call me Manuel," he said politely.

Mateo extended his hand to Manuel. "Hello Manuel, I am Mateo Vega, a business acquaintance of Mr. Peña. Nice to meet you," Mateo said. Manuel shook his hand and sat down while Fernando waved the waitress over for a drink. "Can I get you a beverage, Manuel?" Fernando asked. "Water, please, I don't drink alcohol," Manuel replied.

Mateo smiled and looked at Fernando, confusing the young rapper with the curious exchange. "What?" he asked nervously. Mateo chuckled. "Can you tell us why you don't drink alcohol, Manuel?" Mateo asked, glancing at Fernando.

The young rapper glanced back and forth between the two businessmen, unsure of how to answer, but his honest response spilled out. "I lose focus. Alcohol makes me feel out of control. I don't find it useful in my life, and I'm trying to make that paper. Alcohol is a hindrance; nothing good would come from it," Manuel stated.

Mateo nodded in agreement. "I like you, Manuel. A man after my own heart. I choose to stay away from alcohol as well. Some people find that strange, but like you, I feel it gets in the way of progress," Mateo said with a reassuring smile.

Fernando gave them both a curious look and waved the waitress over. "Bourbon on the rocks, please. Make it a double," he snickered defiantly. "Now, let's get down to business. We need a studio to hear what you've got. I have reached out to several, but only one has a time slot. Next Friday at 3:00, Cash Davidson Studios in Buckhead. That will keep us here for another week, but it's the first available slot. Their equipment is unmatched, and the room acoustics are five-star. I feel like we'll get quality sound and a true sense of your talent. Can you make it?" Fernando asked.

Mateo felt the pieces fall into place. The seed was planted, and Fernando played right into his hands. Mateo would find a way to get the answers he was looking for from Cash and find Camille in the process. A meeting of circumstance is how he would make it all appear.

****

Camille and Cash cruised through the bustling city before hitting the interstate south. "Where are we going? I have asked a thousand times, and you still will not answer me; you're making me nervous," Cami said anxiously.

"You'll see; be patient and just wait for it," Cash replied with a knowing grin. He reached over and placed his hand on Camille's knee, reassuring her with his protective nature.

As they exited the highway, the surroundings began to look familiar to Cami. They entered a suburban neighborhood she recognized from her childhood. Cash pulled into the driveway of 1708 Janie Drive. The driveway was broken and cracked from tree roots, and the house sat empty with a "For Sale" sign in the front yard. Cash came to a complete stop and looked over at Cami lovingly. "Want to take a trip down memory lane?" he asked.

Cami sat in the SUV, staring at her childhood home before slowly emerging. Memories flashed through her mind of the day she moved in, recalling a young Cash Davidson carrying a box of albums to his mother's car. She remembered staring at him, with his dark hair, pink polo shirt, white shorts, and stylish blonde tips. She had felt an instant crush on the 15-year-old boy who stood in front of her without uttering a word.

Cash walked around the vehicle and grabbed her hand. As they walked up the driveway, Cami noticed the familiar handprints etched in the concrete, marked "1982" with the initials "CD." Cash knelt down, placing his hand in the handprint. "Wow, I can't believe this is still here," he said. "Perfect fit," Cami chuckled. "That print has stood the test of time; it was here when I moved in," Cami added, feeling a sense of nostalgia.

"Come on, let's take a look around before the real estate agent gets here," Cash said. Cami stared at him with a curious grin. "Real estate agent? Why have you called a real estate agent?" she asked.

Cash grabbed her hand. "Because I want him to unlock the main house so we can see the inside. Come on, we have about 45 minutes," he said, putting his arm around her waist.

Cash led Cami to the back of the house where a modest pool house sat, lonely and abandoned. Cami's eyes welled with tears, and she began to cry uncontrollably. Cash immediately embraced her. "Wait, don't cry. This is supposed to be a happy moment, sweetheart, not sad. Why are you crying?" he asked, comforting her.

Cami placed her face in her hands, falling into Cash's chest as she poured her heart out. "I am the reason this house sits lonely and abandoned. My mother didn't want to be here alone without me and the children, so she sold it and followed me to Miami. Now she's in that condo in Atlanta with no yard, nowhere to plant her garden, no pool for us to enjoy, and nowhere for my future grandkids to visit. I've just made a mess of everything," she sobbed uncontrollably.

Cash held her close, rubbing the back of her head, feeling the breakthrough he had been looking for. But then Cami quickly wiped her tears away and shut down. She pulled away from Cash. "What are we doing here, Cash?" she asked bluntly.

Cash stepped back, holding her steady by her arms. "I just wanted us to see the place again together. The past is the past. No need to say anymore. Let's just take a stroll around the house, maybe step inside the pool house for some hot sex, and let the real estate agent show us around when he arrives. Nothing more," Cash said with a smile.

Cami began to laugh. "I have such a thing for corny men, but hot sex with a cornball in the pool house sounds fun," she said with a playful grin and wet tears on her face.

Cash pulled out a handkerchief from his pocket and began to wipe Cami's tears. She pulled away, teasing, "Do you blow your nose with that thing?"

Cash busted out in laughter. "Every day," he said, still chuckling. They stared at each other, a shared smile lingering between them. Suddenly, Cash lifted her up, and her legs instinctively wrapped around his waist as he walked her to the unlocked pool house. Inside, he laid her down on a strategically placed blow-up mattress, LED candles lighting the area, and fresh flowers scattered about.

Cash sauntered to a vintage record player, placing the needle on an old Bon Jovi album and letting it play. Cami looked around and smiled, deciding to save her questions for later. They embraced in a passionate kiss, slowly removing each other's clothing. It felt like they were teenagers meeting for the first time in a familiar, comfortable space. The music set the tone, evoking nostalgic memories of their childhood. Two perfectly matched strangers, sharing parallel memories for so many years, now found themselves together. It all felt so surreal.

****

Cami and Cash lay back on the blow-up mattress in the silk sheets that Cash had placed there in their old pool house surrounded by familiarity. Cami lifted her head from his pounding chest, her hair slightly hanging in her face. "How in the hell did you set this up, and what are we really doing here? There is no real estate agent coming, is there?" she inquired.

Just then, Cash remembered that his good friend, a local realtor, would be there any minute. "Oh shit," Cash jumped up, peeping out of the small window of the pool house. He saw Grant Alford walking through the gate. "Shit, get your clothes on. I'll handle him," Cash said in a hurry, throwing on his white collared button-up, quickly tucking it into his jeans, and sliding his shoes on.

Cami pulled the sheets over her naked body. "Cash, are you kidding me?" she whispered loudly.

"No," he said as he hurried out of the pool house, meeting Grant halfway.

"What's up, man? I didn't think you were coming," Cash stated, surprised.

"And why is that? I'm only 20 minutes late," Grant said, looking over Cash's shoulder, catching a glimpse of Cami slipping on her clothes and shuffling her hair. "Cash, what the hell, man? Are you messing around with someone in there? Jesus, I could lose my license. What if another agent or curious buyers happen to walk up? How would I explain this? When you asked me for the key to the pool house, I thought you were just checking out the place and I would meet you here. You have an entire setup in there. It looks like you have moved in!" Grant stated angrily.

"I know, man, listen, I have a wild story about this place, and I want to buy it. So no worries, how much?" Cash asked, excited.

Grant furrowed his brow at Cash. "Are you serious? Cash, this place needs a lot of work. It's been sitting here for about three years. It needs leveling; the pool needs a new liner, a new roof, and kitchen appliances. I've been waiting for an investor to buy it, to be honest. Man, you don't want this house. The last couple that bought it let it go into foreclosure after a year because they couldn't afford all the repairs," Grant said, trying to save his friend the trouble.

Cash looked at Grant, feeling aggravated. "I am an investor. How much? They don't call me Cash for no reason. I'll pay cash. How much?" Cash insisted.

Just then, Cami came strolling out of the pool house, her head held high, trying to play it cool and offering her hand as an introduction. "Hi, I am Camille," she said, purposely leaving out her last name.

Grant kept a suspicious look on his face. "Grant Alford, Peachtree Realty. You from around here?" he asked curiously.

Cami stood silent for a moment, fearing that Grant might recognize her from a headline in Miami. She quickly gathered her thoughts and, in her best southern accent, replied, "Of course. Matter of fact, this was my childhood home. I grew up right here in this very spot," she stated confidently.

"Didn't you go to school around here?" Grant asked.

"Yes, I did, but you wouldn't know me. I was very quiet and didn't hang with a lot of people," Cami said sheepishly.

Grant shook his head at the memory. "Oh, I remember you, Camille Leone, right?" he asked.

"Yes," Cami said shyly.

"Yeah, that's you. I always felt bad for you, sitting by yourself, always so quiet. Pretty but quiet. Kind of a mystery to most of us horny boys. We all thought you were mean. Must have been your green eyes," Grant said flirtatiously.

Cash caught on to the conversation. "Okay, Grant, that's enough. Let's get down to business. We didn't go to school with Camille," Cash stated assuredly.

Grant looked at Cash and smirked. "You didn't, but oh, I did. Just a few years of high school. You were in private school, Cash, running around with the rich girls while we poor kids toughed it out in public school. Cami here went out with Danny Cruz for a while," Grant said, shaking his head at the memory.

Cami stood shocked by what this stranger knew about her but was relieved it was nothing recent. "Yes, I did. He was my high school sweetheart for a while. A lot of wild memories from that era, so to speak. Good memory you have," Cami said, smiling.

"You weren't easy to forget, Ms. Leone," Grant said softly.

Cash was taken aback by Grant's boldness. "Hey, snap out of it, Grant. I'm standing here, motherfucker," Cash stated, only half-jokingly, but his aggravation was evident. "Now tell me, how much is the house?" Cash asked again.

Cami's mouth dropped open, shocked by the question. "What do you mean, how much, Cash?" she asked.

"Yes, Cami, I want to buy this house. For me, of course, if you choose to live here after the divorce is final, I thought maybe we could make it a project together. Bring it back to life," Cash said romantically as he leaned over to kiss her.

Cami, still taken aback by the gesture, laughed and dropped her head, trying to fight back tears. A man giving her life back that she had so quickly given up for Mateo. She raised her head and wrapped her arms around Cash. "I think that is a great idea, Cash Davidson. I love you," she said unexpectedly. Cash stared at Camille, surprised at how natural her response was. His heart filled with pride, knowing that he had won her love.

Chapter 19

One Week Later

Mateo and Fernando met for breakfast at a local Cuban bakery in downtown Atlanta. Mateo sat confidently, placing his white napkin in his lap and sipping on freshly squeezed orange juice. Fernando ordered his morning special mimosa and a bowl of fruit while the men waited for their hearty breakfast to arrive.

"You're getting started early, I see, Fernando," Mateo said, reminding Fernando of his disdain for alcohol.

"Nothing like a mimosa and fresh fruit on this muggy Georgia morning," Fernando chuckled.

The two men laughed lightly at their differences when they were interrupted by a beautiful redheaded waitress. "Good morning, gentlemen; what can I get you?" she asked softly.

The two men exchanged glances. Fernando leaned in, "Not me, brother. I'm done with redheads. You can have this one," he whispered, reminding Mateo of where all his troubles began with Scarlett Cox.

"I'll pass," Mateo whispered back, then looked at the confused waitress and smiled. "I'll have scrambled eggs, refried beans and crème, fried plantains, and mango on the side."

Fernando, frustrated with the menu choices, said, "I'll have the same. Thank you, Bonita."

"Careful, Fernando, that looks like flirting to me," Mateo laughed.

"So, did you set everything up with the studio?" Mateo asked.

Fernando lit his cigar, billowing smoke flowing from his lips. "I did. I spoke with Cash Davidson this morning. He confirmed the open space for tomorrow at 3 pm. He's going to meet us at the studio and let us in. We may be able to utilize him for future producing as well," Fernando stated assuredly.

"Perfect," Mateo responded. A rush of adrenaline ran through his veins. His plan was executing itself as if the stars had aligned once again. He was one step closer to finding Cami. She had been a ghost for close to two years, silent on social media, no communication with anyone in Miami until that fateful call to Ashley Strong. Mateo was confident that he would get his answers from Cash Davidson.

Friday Morning

Cash and Cami held each other tightly, watching the morning news, when an image of Beau and Salty appeared on the screen. The journalist started to speak, and both Cami and Cash sat up, listening intently.

"Atlanta's local artists, born and bred right here in Atlanta, sold out a show at Madison Square Garden last night, opening up for none other than underground hip-hop sensation turned country rap stars J-Boy and Black Hat Nation," the journalist exclaimed as the screen showed the two familiar artists rapping their latest hit on stage.

Cami placed her hands over her mouth, shocked and elated for her old friend and once-lover. Cash jumped out of bed and headed for the phone, immediately calling Beau and screaming into the phone when he answered.

"What's up, motherfucker! Holy shit, y'all made it, dude. I am so proud of you. Why didn't you tell me you were opening up for J-Boy and Black Hat Nation?" Cash exclaimed.

"Man, we didn't know it was going to happen so fast. We got out to Cali last week and met up in the studio on the first day; they liked our work, we collaborated, and the next thing we knew, we went from underground to a worldwide stage. It's been a whirlwind experience—East Coast to West Coast back to East Coast in just a few weeks. But look, we didn't forget you, man. Matter of fact, I was waiting for you to call me," Beau said intently.

"Oh really? Well, damn, man, I would have called sooner, but I've been tied up. This divorce has been a bitch, but Cami set me up with a great attorney from Miami who is collaborating with another attorney here in Georgia. Hopefully, we'll get this shit behind us. It's worked out pretty well for us so far—few bumps here and there, but we've made it," Cash said confidently, smiling at Cami sitting on his bed, waiting to congratulate her old friend.

"Congratulations, Beau. I am so proud of you. You deserve every bit of it. Tell Salty hello for me," Cami exclaimed as Cash held out the phone for Beau to hear.

Beau sat in silence for a moment, surprised to hear Cami's voice but happy to know she was there with Cash. "Thank you, Cami. I am happy to hear you two are doing well. Remember, don't let anything steer you from what is real," Beau said lovingly.

Cami and Cash furrowed their brows and looked at the phone. "Um, okay, that sounds like solid advice, Beau. I'll be sure to remember that," Cami said sarcastically, then silently gestured to Cash with her arms and mouthed, "I don't know what that means." Cash put the phone back to his ear and changed the subject, getting all the latest tour dates and information. When he hung up, he approached Cami.

"What was that about, Camille?" Cash asked, his tone concerned.

"I have absolutely no idea, Cash. I truly don't know where that came from," Cami said honestly.

"Well, anyway, I have to get ready to go to the studio. I have a couple of clients that I am meeting at 3 o'clock, and I don't want to be late. I would like to work with this new artist," Cash said as he hurried to the shower.

Cami watched him, his thin muscular frame and salt-and-pepper hair exuding maturity. She started to feel a throbbing between her legs as she watched him prepare to shave his afternoon shadow. "Come back to bed for a minute, baby," Cami called out.

"Oh no, coming back to bed with you is way more than a minute. I have some errands to run before I meet them, and I am not going to be late. I have a schedule, and if it's interrupted, my whole day is fucked. I'm a Libra, baby; you can't tip my scales," Cash said jokingly.

"But I miss you already, and I have the day off. Please, just one minute," Cami begged.

Cash peeped his head around the corner of the bathroom, his face filled with shaving cream, his abs tight and naturally tan. He smiled at her. "Why don't you go with me?" he asked.

"Really?" Cami exclaimed.

"Why not? A beautiful woman on your arm is always a way to seal the deal," Cash said as he watched Cami quickly jump out of bed and head for the shower.

****

Beau hung up the phone, shook his head, and scoffed. "What was that about? Was that Cash and Cami I heard?" Salty asked curiously.

"Yeah, man, that was Cash and Cami. But do you remember when we were on the escalator in Atlanta, leaving for California?" Beau asked.

"Yeah, man. We saw that dude she left you for, Mateo, and that Fernando cat we played for in Miami, the one Cami was with on her birthday," Salty explained.

"Yeah, that guy. Well, I just knew in the back of my mind he was looking for Cami, and I was sure Cash would be an emotional wreck by now. But oddly, they seem fine. I guess he hasn't found her yet," Beau said, chuckling.

"Well, did you fucking tell him that motherfucker is in town?" Salty exclaimed.

"Fuck no, he doesn't even know that dude exists. I am not getting involved. He will know soon enough because if Mateo is looking for her, he will find her, and I don't want any part of that shit. I'll just be there to pick up the pieces with Cash after Mateo sweeps her right back off her feet. I'll meet him at that station once he gets off that Crazy Train, if you know what I mean," Beau said casually, laughing and lighting his blunt, then handing it to Salty.

"Yeah, man, fuck that Crazy Train. I'm not buying a ticket for that shit," Salty exclaimed, watching the smoke tendrils whirl in the air and contemplating a new song. "Hey man, we should write a song and call it 'Crazy Train.' I can already hear it in my head," Salty exclaimed.

 "Yeah, man," Beau said as he sat and stared out of the window, down at the bustling streets of New York, struggling with his emotions. He was torn between saving his friend Cash from what he thought was to come or keeping his promise to Cami.

****

Cami and Cash pulled up to the studio an hour early. The anticipation was electric as Cami thought about experiencing everything Cash loved—Music! As Cash unlocked the door and led her inside, she was greeted by a sprawling studio filled with buttons, sound booths, and microphones. It was like stepping into a different world.

"So, what do you think?" Cash asked, watching Cami as she stood in awe.

"Wow, this is a bit overwhelming. How do you know what buttons to push?" Cami asked, her fingers lightly grazing the large anatomy of the studio mixing board.

Cash positioned himself on the corner of the board, a playful grin on his face. "The same way you know how to push my buttons," he said fervently, leaning in to kiss her chest and pressing his hands against her breast.

Cami burst into laughter. "You really are witty and funny and sometimes corny, but it really turns me on," she said, embracing him passionately.

"Give me one minute," Cash said sarcastically, biting her ear and circling it with his tongue.

"Oh no, remember, a minute is not one minute with me. Besides, your clients will be here in 45 minutes. I don't want to smell like sex. You know men pick up on that," Cami stated firmly.

"Not if it's only one minute. Just call me the minute, man—in and out, you know, a quickie. I'm so horny right now, Camille. Just give it to me," Cash said, his breath ragged and desperate.

"The minute-man, is that what you want me to call you?" Cami said, laughing. Her authentic laughter was contagious, and it made Cash's heart swell as he joined in, loving their shared humor.

"I love to see you laugh, Cami. You know, I don't think I've ever seen you truly laugh before. I feel so good about us at this moment. I love you to the moon and back," Cash said sincerely. Pulling a small box from his pocket, Cash opened it to reveal a silver necklace with a diamond moon pendant. Cami gave him an endearing smile. "I love it, Cash. It's perfect," she said, turning around so he could place it around her neck.

Cami gave him a quick peck on his lips, locking eyes with him. "I love you more," she said, her voice full of warmth and sincerity.

Cash smiled, feeling truly loved for the first time. "I've dreamed of a woman like you, Cami. It's like God just handed you to me. Do you really want to be with me? Sometimes I worry that if it seems too good to be true, it probably is," he said, his eyes meeting the floor as he waited for her response.

Cami lightly lifted his chin, her touch gentle. "Look, if I didn't want to be here with you, I wouldn't be. If I didn't want to help you with this divorce, I wouldn't. And if I didn't want to renovate our childhood home together, well, I wouldn't do that either. But I do want to because it's going to be so much fun. I can't wait to tell Mom—she's going to be so excited. And speaking of my mother, I would like for you to meet her," Cami said.

Cash smiled, feeling more confident. "Oh, so it's time to meet the folks, huh? Well, I'm down. The sooner, the better. That's always a good sign, you know, meeting the parents," he said.

"I love you, Cash Davidson. I'm in this now. Let's go meet your clients. This is going to be interesting. I'm so excited; I feel like I'm going to have an anxiety attack," Cami said, laughing as she took a deep breath.

"Calm down, sweetheart. We're going to meet them in my office first and then head down here. Let's head upstairs first. Maybe you'll let me have that minute on my desk," Cash said, slowly rubbing between Cami's legs.

"No, emphatically no. Now, let's go," Cami said, pulling Cash toward the elevators. The couple flirted and teased each other all the way to Cash's office, blissfully unaware of the unfolding treachery ahead.

****

Mateo and Fernando waited in the valet section for their driver. Mateo, dressed in bright red pants and a white button-up shirt, left open to reveal a skull necklace given to him by Cami for his birthday; wearing it gave him a sense of freedom without Esme's constant nagging. This moment made him feel closer to Cami. His wavy black hair was perfectly styled, and the line of his goatee was sharp and precise. Fernando stood next to him, handsome in his own right but heavier set, resembling a middle-aged mob boss with large-rim sunglasses, a three-piece suit, and a cigar. Both were excited about the day's events but for very different reasons.

They eagerly stepped into the blacked-out SUV. Mateo stared out of the window, lost in his thoughts during the 20-minute drive to the studio, feeling closer to Cami with each passing minute.

"Why so quiet, Mateo? What's on your mind?" Fernando asked curiously.

Mateo snapped out of his daydream and quickly changed his demeanor. "Oh, just missing Victor," he said.

"At least you get to see your little mijo. Scarlett gives me a hard time, and between her and my wife, they're about to drain me financially. I need this deal to come through. We need this artist on board," Fernando said, his frustration palpable.

"He will be on board; I will make sure of it," Mateo replied determinedly.

The driver slowly pulled into the parking lot, letting the two men out at the three-story building. Mateo and Fernando made their way inside, peering through the black windows of the studio.

"I don't see anyone," Mateo remarked.

"I'll call Cash," Fernando said, dialing his number.

Cash answered on the first ring. "Hello. Cash Davidson," Cash announced himself.

"Si, Señor, we're downstairs by the studio. Where are you?" Fernando questioned.

"Upstairs, third floor in my office. I figured we'd talk first, have a bourbon, and discuss expectations and pricing," Cash replied.

"Sounds good; we are on the way up," Fernando responded. The two men stepped onto the elevator, their excitement building, and pressed the button for the third floor.

Cash hung up and looked at Camille. "They're on their way up," Cash explained.

Cami smiled. "Okay, I'm going to go to the bathroom, freshen up, and I'll be right back. I like looking my best for you, baby," she said teasingly.

"You would look good in a paper sack," Cash teased back.

Cami walked into the bathroom clutching her small handbag, her green maxi dress hugging her curvaceous body. She began applying her gloss and lipstick in the mirror, flipping her full black hair over her shoulder. Suddenly, she heard the office door open and the sound of introductions, feeling a faint recognition of one of the muffled voices.

Unaware, she walked out of the bathroom, head down while adjusting her lipstick in the side pocket of her clutch bag, she heard Cash speaking. "Ah, there she is, my beautiful princess. Cami, meet Mateo Vega and Fernando Pena."

Cami slowly lifted her head. Her eyes met Mateo's, and her skin felt flush as he smiled at her. Cash's voice became an echo as she tried to compose herself, her hands beginning to shake until she dropped her small handbag. Mateo quickly leaned in to pick it up and handed it to her. "Hi, Camille. I never imagined I would see you again," Mateo said as he handed her the bag.

Cash stood there, confused by the familiarity between the two. Fernando cut his eyes at Mateo but knew not to utter a word. "Hi, Mateo. Hope you are well. How is your wife and son?" Cami asked with a half-smile.

"Cami, she is not my wife, but Esme is, well, you know.... she is Esme. And Victor is growing, walking, and talking now," Mateo answered with a smile.

Cash was speechless until he finally asked, "You two know each other?"

Cami took a deep, shaky breath. "Yes, Cash, this is my ex-husband, Mateo Vega," she said, looking down at the ground.

"Oh, wow, I had no idea. So, did you know he was coming here?" Cash asked inquisitively.

"No, I did not, Cash. And had I known he would be here, I would have stayed in bed today," Cami said as she started to walk out the door, practically running while fighting back tears and repeating Beau's last words in her head. *Remember, Cami, what is real.*

The three men let her go as Mateo looked at Cash. "I apologize. I had no idea you two were acquainted. I came here for business and could have never expected to see her here. I have not spoken to Camille or seen her for nearly two years, so you can imagine what a surprise this is for both of us," Mateo said, feeling the daggers from Fernando's glare.

"I can imagine, Mr. Vega. She has never mentioned you. So, you can understand what a shock this is for me as well," Cash stated intently.

"Oh, is that so?" Mateo inquired.

"That is so, Mr. Vega. Not one word," Cash said, locking eyes with Mateo.

Mateo drew in a breath and politely asked, "Would you mind if I walked down and spoke with her before we get started?"

Cash picked up his phone from his desk and dialed Camille's number. He knew she couldn't be far since she had ridden with him to the studio. She quickly answered, "Cash, I am so sorry. I had no idea he was the one you were meeting. This is my past, right there in 3D, standing before you. There is so much I need to tell you, but I wanted to wait until the time was right," Cami clamored for her words.

"It's okay, princess. Mr. Vega has asked to speak with you privately. Will you grant him that request, or should I tell him no? I can call you an Uber to get you home if you don't wish to stay," Cash offered.

Cami wanted so badly to be strong, but Mateo's pull was intoxicating. She knew she loved Cash and that Mateo would not win her over, but she wanted to see him in a sick way she couldn't deny. "That is fine. I am down here in the studio. I will give him ten minutes only if you are okay with it," Cami stated.

"I trust you, princess. I am okay with it. I will send him down," Cash said lovingly as he hung up. He looked over at Mateo hesitantly, his dark skin and dapper appearance even intimidating to the very fit, more mature Cash Davidson. "Mr. Vega, Camille says she will give you ten minutes in the studio. Nothing more, nothing less," Cash stated with hesitation.

Mateo slightly tilted his head in a gesture of thanks and quickly headed for the studio. Mateo stepped off the elevator and walked slowly to the studio door, where he began peering through the small window of the door, robbing himself of time with her just to look at her in silence as she wiped away tears rolling down her cheek. Mateo slowly opened the door.

"Camille, how are you, Amor?" he asked.

Cami drew in a deep breath as she stared at the floor. She could smell him from across the room. Cami began to talk to herself, "He is not real," she whispered lightly. She finally found the courage to lift her head and look him in the eye. As their eyes locked, every thought of running and every word she had rehearsed left her body. In two steps, she wrapped her arms around his neck, and they embraced each other in silence, feeling their hearts pounding in unison. Mateo's eyes welled with tears that slowly fell down his cheeks.

"Mi Amor, I've missed you every day," he whispered.

Camille lay her head on Mateo's chest, inhaling the familiar scent of his cologne. It was a smell that always reminded her of their undeniable connection. "Camille, I am so very sorry to interrupt your life like this, but I have missed you desperately," he murmured, taking her tear-streaked face in his hands. "I know that you still love me. I know that you want to be home with me, back in Miami. When I heard the faint sound of your voice during your call with Ashley Strong, I couldn't help but come looking for you," Mateo recalled.

"Wait, did Ashley tell you who I was with?" Camille asked angrily.

"No, Camille, she did not. In fact, she was adamant about not telling me anything, but I saw her write Cash's name down, so I started to look for you. You've been so elusive—no social media, no clues. I had no idea you would be here today, but I thought if I could get close to Cash, I would find you. You don't have to answer me now, but please think about coming back with me. We can start over. I'll buy you a new home. I have legitimized Victor and obtained the rights to my son, and I am working to be rid of Esme," he proclaimed.

The mention of Esme and Victor gave Camille her resolve. She quickly pulled away just as Cash hurried through the door, Fernando close behind. Camille and Mateo locked eyes with Cash as he announced his presence. "Camille, what is going on here?" Cash inquired, then turned angrily to Mateo. "You've had your ten minutes, Mr. Vega," he stated, his anger palpable.

Camille sniffled and lightly shook her head, filled with guilt at the thought of returning to Mateo. Cash, realizing the meeting must have been arranged by Mateo, felt warnings from Beau resurface in his mind. He turned to Fernando. "Was this set up? You don't really have business here," Cash stated angrily.

Fernando hesitantly approached Cash. "That is not true, Mr. Davidson. I had no idea that Camille would be here or that you two were acquainted," Fernando stated innocently, looking to Mateo for answers.

Mateo began to confess. "Cash, may I call you Cash?" he asked.

Cash, aggravated by the formality, replied, "Yes, get on with it."

"Cash, as you now know, Camille is my ex-wife. My indiscretions and mine alone have brought us to this place. I do not come here to interrupt her life, but simply to make amends for what I have done to her," Mateo was interrupted by Camille's protest.

"Please, Mateo, just stop," she said gently.

Mateo continued, "Mr. Pena and I have legitimate business with you, but I will confess that I knew Camille might have been in a lengthy relationship. My fear has always been that she will move on before giving me the chance to apologize and see if the deep connection we have for each other is still there," he said truthfully.

Cash looked at Camille, who stood staring at the floor, bracing herself against a small table. "So, Camille, what do you want to say? End this with this man, and let's get on with our lives. They have both wasted my time, your time, and that of several artists who could have been here today. I will not stand here another minute allowing this man to question the love that you and I share nor threaten our plans for the future," Cash stated defiantly.

Camille closed her eyes, biting her bottom lip in disbelief that it was happening all over again and that Mateo's pull was as strong as ever. "Cash, it's not that easy; I have tried for years.

I do love you unconditionally and would never want to hurt you or leave you," Camille confessed.

Cash began to realize his worst fears, interrupting Camille before she could finish. "So he was right?" Cash said with clarity.

Camille raised a brow in confusion. "Who was right?" she asked.

Cash shook his head, the realization of Beau's words coming to pass. "Beau. He told me to guard myself from you, from this entire situation. He said he didn't know anything about Miami, but he knew. He was protecting you by not telling me. You sure have these men wrapped around your finger, it appears," Cash said knowingly.

"Cash, I have not said that I am going with him. This is just very complicated," Camille pleaded.

Cash placed his hands on his hips, his strong jaw clenching at Camille's words. "Complicated? You mean to tell me after nearly a year of being together, sharing what we have, this man can walk in, and in a matter of minutes, you're confused again? Complicated, you say?" Cash asked, cutting Camille off and giving her no opportunity to answer. "I tell you what, you and your ex-husband here, get the fuck out of my studio. Go find yourselves, rekindle this so-called love that you two have for each other that has obviously not worked in the past, and try it again. But don't come knocking on my door for comfort when it falls apart. Because, like Beau, I will deny you," Cash said angrily and walked out, slamming the studio door behind him.

Fernando looked at Mateo in disappointment before following Cash back to his office. Mateo cautiously approached Camille, attempting to rub her hair, but she angrily pushed his hand away, wiping her tears.

"You enjoy this, don't you, Mateo?" Camille seethed. "My happiness is of no consequence to you. You don't care that I am moving on. It is your mission to destroy me!" she screamed.

"Camille, that is not true," Mateo said, trying to touch her face to calm her.

"Don't fucking touch me!" Camille snapped, swiping his hand away once again.

"Please, Camille, just a couple of hours. I know that you have never stopped loving me. I can feel you in my soul. I know that I have been unfaithful, but there is no woman who will ever take your place," Mateo begged, holding his hand out toward her. "Come with me, just for a couple of hours."

Camille stared at Mateo, remembering the infidelity, the legal issues, and how she hurt Beau. Despite feeling captivated, she thought of Cash and their deep bond. "No, Mateo, I will not. I love you, I will always love you, but I can't do this to him. Please leave," she kindly asked.

Mateo dropped his hand, his disappointment evident. "You know where to find me, Camille. If you come back to Miami, I will have a place for us. No Esme, I promise," he stated clearly.

"Mateo, if you want to be done with her, be done, but don't do it on my account," Camille said with a steady tone.

Mateo shook his head in defeat, handing Camille his business card. She looked at the card and smirked. "Music producer? Really, Mateo? You will never quit, will you?" Camille asked.

Mateo gave her a half-smile. "Never," he said knowingly.

Chapter 20

Four Hours Later

Camille lightly closed the door to her home, emotionally defeated by the day's events. She flopped down in the leather Victorian-style chair nestled by the window in the corner of her living room and let out an exhausted breath. She placed her hands on the ornate details of the arms, scaling the entirety of the room as she recalled Mateo's heartfelt apology for years of discord and the heated exchange between him and Cash. The sound of Cash's F-150 pulling into the driveway snapped her back to reality. She turned slowly, sliding her fingers between the blinds to watch him drive in. She remained seated, waiting for the inevitable confrontation.

She heard the keys in the lock, and as Cash walked in, his face appeared relieved that she was still there. He slowly approached Camille, who seemed frozen in her chair. Cash dropped to his knees and placed his face in her lap, rubbing her thighs with his strong hands. Camille ran her fingers through his hair, their silence speaking volumes.

Not a word was uttered as he lifted her dress and started to kiss the inside of her thighs, his hands caressing her waist before moving up to feel her stomach and gently lifting her dress over her head. He stood up and looked her in the eye, where she sat naked, waiting for him to take her. Waiting to feel that passion she once felt when Mateo took her. She closed her eyes, hoping that fire would ignite and she would forget that Mateo had even been there.

Before she knew it, Cash lifted her out of the chair and carried her to the bedroom. They made love for hours, never speaking a word.

Later that evening, Cash emerged from an emotionally exhausting day and a deep sleep, having spent hours in passionate intimacy. He found Cami sitting in the chair once again, wrapped in her white silk robe, her black hair flowing over her barely showing breast, staring out of the window, lost in her thoughts.

"Hey, are you ok?" Cash asked softly.

Cami looked up at him and smiled at the sweet man she had spent the last year with, the one who was enough for her to deny Mateo.

"Yes, for now I am," she said quietly.

"For now? Don't you think we should talk about what happened today? I was surprised to see you here when I arrived. I surely thought you would have left with him," Cash said with certainty.

Cami gave him a half smile. "No, I did not leave with him. I had no plans of doing so," she stated.

"I surely thought after your reaction to him I would be left on the island," Cash said, chuckling.

Cami chuckled with him. "I love you, Cash, but do you think we moved too fast? I mean, your divorce is not even final. There's no telling how long this family will drag it out. I've never healed from this very toxic relationship. Don't you think we should have taken it a bit slower, maybe fixed ourselves first?" Cami asked honestly.

Cash braced himself against the wall, staring at the ceiling, looking for the words, and preparing himself for what he knew was coming. "No, Camille, I do not think we moved too fast. I think we found each other at the perfect time in what we thought was a hopeless place. But I can tell where this is going, and I don't like it," his voice trembling.

Cami slowly got up, adjusting her robe, and approached Cash. "I love you very much, but I need to heal. I have been thinking about something really long and hard. I have made the decision to go to Italy and be with Gabriella. Away from here for a while. I need to find myself, love myself again so that I can properly love someone else," she stated with sadness but certainty in her voice.

"Italy? And what will you do in Italy, Camille?" Cash asked, perplexed.

Cami smirked, feeling Cash's emotions. "Gabriella is teaching English. Maybe I could help her or teach school myself. Maybe I could work in a café, hand out towels on the beach, work in a hotel, or a flower shop. There are lots of things I could do. My daughter is there; she misses me, and I need to get away. Wouldn't you rather me be healed from this trauma and be whole again? I'll never be good for anyone if I don't face this and find the meaning of true love. I am not running off with Mateo. Does he stir something in me? Honestly, yes, he does, but this time, it's not love; it's motivation. Do you understand what I am saying, Cash?" Cami asked, desperate for him to understand her.

Cash gently placed both hands on her face, searching for clarity in her eyes. At that moment, he knew she was telling the truth.

Her desire to leave had nothing to do with Mateo or himself. She truly wanted to heal from her trauma and become the best version of herself for someone. He could only hope that, in the end, it would be him.

"Camille, I love you so much. Sometimes, you have to break your own heart to prove your love, and if that means letting you go, then that is what I will do. I understand. I will square up my affairs here, get this divorce, focus on my children, and heal myself. But promise me you will come back to me," he said as he lightly kissed her on the forehead.

Cami remembered the old house Cash had purchased, the one they both had so many plans for and memories of as children. "What are you going to do with the house?" she asked with curiosity.

"Well, I bought it for us. Grant has written the contract. I'm going to fix it up, and if you decide to return it to me, it will be here waiting for you. Maybe I could still meet your mom, and she could help me," Cash said, hope filling his words.

Camille felt her chest tighten. The kindness of his words and his plans for their future were heartbreaking considering her decision, but she remained steadfast. "I'm sorry, Cash. I have to do this, and I have to do this without a plan. I need to find my purpose, and I realized today that I don't know my purpose because I look for men to give me that," she said, rubbing his smooth face, admiring his gentleness and maturity.

Cash knowingly shook his head and walked into the bedroom, standing in silence, heartbroken by her decision. "I will miss you, Princess," he said as he started to gather his belongings.

Cami followed close behind, uncontrollable tears flowing down her face. "I hope we find each other again. I will not be gone forever. You know, a good friend once told me that when love is real, it will always find its way back to you," she said tearfully as he walked out of the door and out of her life.

Two Weeks Later

Camille rolled her luggage through Hartsfield International Airport and walked into the Delta Sky Lounge. She gave the bartender a soft smile and placed her order. "Can I get a glass of Merlot, please?" The bartender nodded and obliged her with a proper pour of house Merlot.

Cami sipped on her glass, hoping to calm her nerves from the pending flight. Just then, a gentleman took a seat next to her. Camille felt a bit uncomfortable but smiled at the man before using her phone as a distraction, scrolling through Instagram.

"Vacation?" he asked curiously.

Camille smirked, thinking of her impending trip and her thoughts of the future. "No, this is a business trip," she said bluntly, sipping her glass of red wine.

"Oh, really? Where are you doing business, if you don't mind me asking?" the man queried.

Camille took another long sip of her Merlot and hesitantly answered her curious admirer.

"Miami."

To be continued…

****

Made in the USA
Columbia, SC
27 February 2025